I0666854

THE ESCAPADES OF SYLVIA

1st edition © 2010

Author: Sylvia van de Zande

Publisher: Sylvia Erotics.

www.sylviaerotics.com

ISBN: 978-94-90914-02-8

THE ESCAPADES OF SYLVIA

*A*t the end of the summer Sylvia had become rather bored with her job as an office assistant, working through telephone guides and continuously phoning people, trying to persuade them to take out insurance policies they didn't need. After almost a year of the same routine she had decided to explore the market for something more exciting. She had responded to several advertisements and had received some positive reactions. One advert in particular, in her local newspaper, intrigued her and she had decided to follow it up. It was a decision that would lead her to a completely different way of life and would fulfil many of her wildest fantasies.

It was a bright sunny day as she walked through the central area of Rotterdam on her way to her appointment. The advertisement in her newspaper had been small but intriguing and the woman on the telephone had sounded cheerful and enthusiastic. She had taken the Metro to the central station and was following the instructions the woman had given her. She walked along a busy street over a bridge towards a set of traffic lights, passing a large metal artwork structure. At the lights she crossed to the other side of the street and turned into a quiet road lined on one side with sedate houses and on the other with a mixture of shops and small businesses. She passed a dealer in restaurant apparatus, a sign makers shop and a hairdresser. Then she stopped walking as she suddenly noticed a white painted window which was decorated on one side with a silhouette of a woman's face painted in black lacquer. Underneath the face were the words 'Body Line.' This must be the place she thought, as she tried to look inside through the window, but it was completely covered with whitewash. She could hear voices and movements inside. Outside it was very still with not a person in sight.

Feeling a little apprehensive she took a deep breath, pushed the door open and stepped inside. It took several seconds for her eyesight to adjust from the sunlight outside to the dimly lit interior. She was standing next to long bar, and in a large room behind the bar she could see three men. One

3

of them, a young eastern looking man, was busy hanging up a chandelier. He smiled, jumped down from his ladder and walked towards her. 'Welcome to Body Line,' he said enthusiastically, with his hand outstretched. 'I'm Alfred. You must be one of the young ladies interested in our advertisement. You have probably already spoken to my mother. She is in the office. I will call her. Please take a seat.' He spoke quickly and without pause and seemed to be just as nervous as she was. He pointed to a row of stools in front of the bar.

She sat on one of the stools, placed her bag on the counter and began to take in her surroundings. The bar counter was a soft grey colour, edged with brightly polished brass and long enough to serve the twelve red leather stools lined up in front of it. The bar was dimly lit by several red and gold coloured lamps hanging from the ceiling. Suspended between the lamps, was some dark mahogany shelving filled with glasses and bottles. Hanging on the wall behind the bar was a large mirror in an elaborately gilded frame. On each side of the mirror were colourful Chinese looking Buddha's. Bouquets of flowers had been placed strategically on the bar to soften its hard lines. A Hi-FI installation was softly playing background music. The atmosphere was intimate and relaxing.

The floor in front of the bar was covered in a plush dark red carpet that extended into the room beyond. In the corner of the room, almost hidden by the bar, was a group of leather settees arranged around a bronze tinted glass salon table which appeared to be supported by the upturned legs a bronze coloured bear? A rather handsome man was sitting on a stool next to a large palm tree smoking a cigarette. He looked at her but said nothing. The other man was busy assembling a mirror fronted cupboard. Occasionally he paused and smiled at her. Sylvia's uneasy feelings began to fade and her curiosity increased. She had a thousand questions to ask and was keen to meet the mother.

After a few minutes she appeared, a small, rather plump but good looking Indonesian looking woman with black upswept hair and dressed in a black jumper, black leggings and black high heel shoes.

'My name is Anita, and you must be Sylvia,' she said cheerfully, please join me in the office.'

Sylvia followed her into a room in a corner of the lounge area opposite the bar.

'Please take a seat,' Anita pointed to a chair in front of a polished oak desk, while she moved round the desk and sat in a large swivel chair behind it.

'The business is not yet opened?' asked Sylvia, keen to show her interest.

Anita shook her head gently. 'No, our plan is to open next Monday, the sixth of August. Hopefully all the supplies we need will have arrived by then. We are still waiting for bath towels and a few other essentials'

Anita looked at her quizzically. 'You are quite young; do you understand what kind of work it is? Have you had any previous experience?'

Sylvia felt her cheeks redden a little. 'Well I realise that it involves erotic massage and although I haven't worked in this field before I am sure I can handle it. Is that a problem?'

The woman's eyes glanced quickly over her. 'No not really, you are good looking and have an attractive figure and we can soon teach you the essential techniques of massaging. Most important is that you enjoy the work. I get the impression that it will not be problem for you. Do you have a steady boyfriend?'

'No. Not at the moment. I split up with my last boyfriend several months ago.'

'Well, that is better so.' Anita looked relieved. 'The last thing we want is a jealous young man causing a nuisance.'

The woman's eyes began to twinkle. 'The massage rooms are upstairs. Downstairs is the changing room, including lockers and showers, and also a sauna and a whirlpool. It will be your task to promote the use of the facilities and to keep the clients occupied and satisfied.'

She stood up, smiled cheerfully and shook Sylvia's hand. 'I think that you are well suited for the work. I look forward to seeing you on opening day. We expect four other girls as well, so please try to get here by nine-o-clock. We want to show you round the facilities, explain the rules and procedures, and give you a chance to get to know each other before any clients arrive. We plan to open at eleven.'

Almost before she realised it Sylvia was standing outside. She wrinkled her eyes against the bright sunlight, feeling a little confused, but at the same time intrigued. *What have I committed myself to?* She thought to herself. *It had all gone so fast. Can I really handle this sort of work?* There were so many more questions she had meant to ask. Now she must wait another week before her curiosity could be satisfied.

Monday the sixth had arrived. Sylvia had woken early, feeling rather nervous after a restless night's sleep, and had stood for a while before her bedroom mirror in the hope that what she saw would boost her self-confidence. She was not as tall as she would have liked, but this was easily compensated for by wearing high heels. She had a slender, curvaceous figure, with long perfectly formed legs and long, wavy, reddish brown hair. A slight reduction in weight around her tummy might help, she thought, being a little over critical, otherwise she was well satisfied with what she saw.

This morning she took extra care with her make-up. She used subtle colours and an eye liner to accentuate her dark brown eyes, and she sprayed her hair to give it a shine. She used a liberal amount of her favourite perfume. She dressed in a tight fitting red dress, with matching high heel shoes and completed the effect with a gold armband and a gold necklace. She turned around slowly in front of the mirror for a last minute check. She looked very sexy.

For a second time, she crossed the bridge and walked along the now familiar route. Again as she reached her destination she felt her heart beating faster. She paused for a few moments then stepped determinedly through the half open door. She was relieved that the first person she saw was Anita, the Indonesian lady, who was standing at the end of the bar, busy folding up towels. Behind her a young lady with long blond hair, wearing a jumper and leather trousers, was pouring coffee into some cups on the glass table. Three other ladies were sitting on the settees.

'Good morning,' said Sylvia shyly.

'Hallo,' answered Anita cheerfully. 'We have been expecting you. Come! I shall introduce you to the other girls.'

'Ladies, this is Sylvia,' she said loudly, so that she could be heard over the continuous chatter.

A tall, well built, dark skinned girl in a tight fitting red dress stood up to shake her hand. 'My real name is Jasmine,' she said with a big smile, 'but while I am working here I shall use the name Chantal.'

Next to her sat a more mature lady, elegantly dressed, with her blond hair arranged in a pony tail. She gave Sylvia a friendly smile. 'I'm Puck, welcome to the team.'

Another glamorous looking, blond haired lady, wearing a tight fitting jumper and mini-skirt, stood up and extended her hand. 'I'm Laura; I hope that we can be good friends.' She moved sideways to make room. 'Why don't you take a seat?'

Sylvia moved round the coffee table and eased into the space next to Laura. At the same time the woman in the leather trousers poured her a cup of coffee. She seemed to be a friend of Anita and was obviously only helping out. Her name was Jolanda.

Silently Sylvia sipped her coffee, listening to the background chatter and assessing her new environment and the characters she would be working with. She noticed that Laura, the girl sitting next to her, was not quite as young as she had first thought, but she was pretty and had a similar body to herself. The dark skinned girl, Chantal, came from Zaire and, although her knowledge of Dutch was somewhat limited, she had an exuberant and confident manner. Each time Anita had neatly folded a bath towel from the pile she laughed loudly and clapped her hands to the amusement of the other girls. The third lady, Puck, was elegantly dressed but rather solidly built and was the oldest, probably in her late thirties.

They were suddenly distracted by a creaking noise as the office door opened and a small, slender, Indonesian looking, middle aged man came towards them. He was neatly dressed in a dark grey suit and a black shirt.

'Hello everybody, my name is Fred, I am Anita's husband.' He stood still for a few seconds, looking at each of the ladies in turn, as though he were appraising their potential. 'Are all the chickens in the roost?' He asked, looking at his wife.

'One girl has not arrived yet. Marieke. If she is not here in ten minutes we shall begin without her.'

'What a pretty kettle of fish,' he murmured, going to the bar, lighting a cigarette and pouring himself a glass of beer.

Puck, the elegant lady with the blond pony tail had a determined look in her eyes. She was somebody, observed Sylvia, who was experienced and who would love to take control of the proceedings. She talked non-stop and also began to help with the towel folding, giving the impression that she was capable of making a much better job of it.

'The best place to hang the bath robes is downstairs in the changing rooms near the showers. The towels would be better upstairs where the girls can give them to their clients; it helps them to break the ice.' Apparently Puck had already inspected all the facilities.

Laura joined in the conversation. 'The scent of the soap in the showers is rather overpowering. Men don't like that.'

'That's right,' giggled Chantal, 'They would be scared that their wives would notice and become suspicious. And, that's not the only problem.' She continued. 'The massage oil is too fatty and would be difficult for the clients to rinse off.'

The chattering continued and Sylvia noticed that Anita was beginning to lose her patience. The minutes crept by like a slowly moving snail. She poured herself another coffee. She felt like she had been sitting on the settee for hours. She was beginning to doze off and had to force herself to keep alert. Jolanda put her hand in front of her face to hide a yawn. Chantal was curled up against the arm of her seat with her eyes closed.

Suddenly the door was flung open and a whirlwind rushed into the salon. It was Marieke. 'Lousy trams,' she complained, 'I had to wait half an hour. Then I got off at the wrong stop and had to walk half a kilometre.' She threw her coat on a stool and slumped into the remaining space next to Chantal. 'Hope I'm not too late.'

Immediately everybody was wide awake. Fred looked bemused from behind the bar. Anita, looking both annoyed and relieved, stood up and clapped her hands. 'It's time to get moving ladies. I hope you have all brought some nice working outfits with you. We are providing you with white top coats so that you all look respectable when the clients arrive, what you wear underneath is your own choice. Let's go downstairs where you can try them on.'

It was quite chilly in the changing room and Sylvia suddenly began to feel nervous, as she was not used to undressing in front of other women. Bags, underwear and discarded clothes were scattered all over the room and there was a confusing smell of deodorant and perfume in the air. Surreptitiously she looked at the others. They also seemed to be undressing as modestly as possible, but she was amazed at the flamboyance of their underwear and guessed that in some cases it had been selected to distract attention from their less than perfect figures. Puck's figure could best be described as motherly, with a well developed tummy and large rounded breasts. Chantal was rather tall and overpowering, Marieke was much too solid. Only Laura, like herself, was really attractive, being slimly built, with a well shaped torso and long sexy legs.

Gradually the atmosphere changed, everyone was becoming more relaxed, even exhibitionist. It was like the changing room at a fashion show. Sylvia put on black stockings and a maroon coloured erotic panty and bra set edged in black lace. Laura suddenly stood completely naked in front of her and the other girls were in various stages of undressing or dressing. It was becoming a competition in glamour, to see who had the prettiest underwear, who had the highest heels and who was the most sensuous. An air of solidarity was also developing; everyone was either giving or receiving compliments, in an attempt to boost each others self-confidence. This was not the time or place for reality; negative or critical remarks were instinctively not made.

Anita was busy sorting out the white coats, trying to ensure that everyone had the correct size. There was much giggling as they tried them on.

'Makes me feel more like a dentist's assistant than a masseuse,' complained Laura, 'but maybe it will give some guys a kick.'

Chantal stood in front of a large mirror. 'This will spoil my chances,' she complained. 'The men won't be able to see my beautiful breasts and my sexy underwear.'

Sylvia was beginning to relax and enjoy herself, and received admiring remarks about her red and black underwear. In turn, she showed interest in the intricate lacework of Laura's bra and Puck's wonderful embroidered blue body stocking. What surprised her most was the beauty of the black girl, Chantal. Tall and statuesque she seemed to tower over the others, dressed in white lace, high stilettos and with long black curly hair. 'You look gorgeous,' said Laura, spontaneously giving her a kiss on the cheek. Chantal laughed cheerfully, clearly pleased with the compliment.

Only Marieka seemed to be less than happy. Although she tried to join in the chit chat and jolly behaviour, she looked out of place. She realised it and so did the others. She looked pathetic in her silver coloured body stocking that stretched like a tight fitting glove over her generous hips and thighs. Although she was quite young her breasts were large and sagging. The expression on her face was somewhere between dejection and desperation. In a naïve attempt to draw attention to herself she lowered her tights to display her navel which was decorated with several piercings, surrounded by two intricate tattoos. She then displayed her breasts which

10

were also pierced with rings. Laura snorted with astonishment. Anita's eyes opened wide with embarrassment. Puck let out an exclamation of amazement. 'And that's not all' said Marieke, suddenly glowing with enthusiasm from all the attention. 'What you don't know is that, for a while I worked in a SM-club where all the girls had piercings and tattoos. I even had this done,' she lowered her slip and opened her legs slightly. There was an embarrassing silence as everyone stared at the two rows of silver rings. Then Anita burst into a nervous laugh. 'How is that possible? Wasn't it painful?' Marieke shook her head. Enjoying the consternation she had caused.

The ice had now been well and truly broken; everyone was completely relaxed, and they began to talk about their previous experiences, their future plans, how they had tried other kinds of work and the reasons why they were keen to work in such an erotic environment.

'I look forward to teasing all those conceited young guys and getting paid for it,' laughed Laura.

'What other work is available nowadays is boring and only pays peanuts,' said Sylvia. 'And, anyway, I think I have the right assets for this sort of work.'

Even the elegant Puck, the most senior of the group, joined in. 'I worked for a period in an S.M. club,' she said rather sheepishly. 'It was fascinating, but at times it was a bit too extreme. All those strange men, with their weird desires and fetishes. This sort of work is much more relaxing.'

'Ladies! Ladies!' Anita clapped her hands again. 'Please keep on your working outfits and your white coats and join me and Fred upstairs. We want to explain the rules and procedures. Each of you has been allocated a locker where you can keep your personal belongings.' She gave each of them a numbered key.

Sylvia was suddenly back down to earth, as if waking from a dream. *What am I doing here dressed in my underwear, amongst people I hardly know?* She thought to herself. *What have I let myself in for?*

Upstairs they joined Jolanda who was sitting in a corner of one of the settees reading a magazine. Another man had arrived and was sitting on a stool in the middle of the bar. Sylvia realised it was the same handsome man that she had noticed hovering in the background on the day of her interview. He seemed to be looking at her. What could he be thinking about? She looked at him secretly out of the corner of her eyes. He had an air of authority and she guessed his age to be in the early forties. He was well dressed, had dark brown hair and piercing blue eyes. He was well built and suntanned, probably as a result of regular visits to the sun bank. Nobody explained who he was. He surveyed the girls like a sultan in a harem.

Laura followed her gaze. 'He is not a client,' she whispered, 'he is one of the owners, and Jolanda is his partner.'

'Is there more than one owner? Who is really in charge here?' Sylvia was becoming intrigued.

'That's not very clear. It's best to listen to Anita and Fred. Maybe they will explain everything. Here.' Laura handed her a leather bound booklet. 'Fred gave us this to read, it's the programs for the clients'

Sylvia flicked through the pages, reading out loud as though it was a restaurant menu. 'Normal massage 125 euro; massage with the masseuse in the whirlpool 170 euro; body to body for one hour 200 euro. What ridiculous prices. Who would pay so much?'

Puck looked at her disdainfully. 'This is a superior salon, child.' She drew slowly on her cigarette. 'I once worked in a salon in Amsterdam. They ask double these prices and most men were happy to pay. When the door opened at eleven there were already one or two guys waiting outside. That's what it must be like here. But it will take time. We have to build up a reputation.'

'With the help of attractive masseuses with good techniques,' Marieke joined in enthusiastically. 'I'm pretty good at sport massage and have had some formal training. I even have a certificate. After a long day stressed up at the office some men like a physical massage.' To demonstrate, she moved quickly behind Laura and began to massage her neck and shoulders with her strong hands.

Laura winced and gently pushed her arms away. 'It's O.K. but I am not really in the mood for this, I think you are more used to massaging men.'

Anita looked surprised. 'Well, we seem to be discovering some hidden talent. Is there anybody else with similar experience?'

Not to be outdone, Puck responded to the challenge. 'I've been in the business for at least twelve years and know most of the tricks, especially the erotic ones. My clients always leave fully satisfied, and usually come back for more.'

'I have also had several years experience,' said Laura, proudly. 'You can't teach me anything new.'

Sylvia began to realise she was the only beginner and decided to keep a low profile. She could learn much from the others.

Almost unnoticed Fred had appeared next to Anita at the corner of the bar. Sylvia found him a bit creepy. The man had a slightly sinister air and a penetrating look that made her feel uneasy. Maybe it was the unusual combination of his dark skin colour and his light grey eyes. It was difficult to pin down his nationality, probably a mixture of Indonesian and some other eastern ancestry. He wore dark clothes and had black hair flecked with grey. She imagined that he drank too much, smoked too much and went too late to bed. Later she learned that he was a master in baccarat.

'Has everyone read the little brown book?' he asked questioningly, waving a copy in his hand. 'Is everything completely clear?' Laura looked thoughtful and the others shrugged their shoulders.

'What does body-to-body mean?' asked Sylvia, blushing slightly.

'You take your clothes off, as sexily as possible, cover your body with massage oil and sit naked on top of your victim. Then spread oil over his body. Then you glide over his body with your tits and your pussy and at the same time massage him with your hands, you tease him, get him completely aroused and eventually finish him off with your hands. The trick is to keep in control and to delay the finishing off treatment until his time is almost up. It is so simple.' The man drew on his cigarette as if it was the most normal activity in the world. 'Any more questions? Massage with whirlpool, means with the client in the bath. Massage with sauna, means with the client in the sauna. In all cases the objective is to keep him relaxed, happy and eventually satisfied.'

'A simple massage, with you standing next to the massage table,' chuckled Anita. 'That is the easiest for you. Then you are less likely to be pestered. You are in complete control.'

'You mean he is more likely to keep his hands to himself,' remarked Laura.

Fred looked irritated at his wife's interference.

'The client is king,' said Puck loudly, as if her opinion was expected. 'When a man enters the massage parlour he must no longer think about his work, his wife or his family life. He is entering a fantasy world where his tensions will be relieved and his erotic desires will be satisfied.'

Anita listened admiringly, and added, 'so is it ladies. Never ask about his work or his circumstances at home. Who knows? Maybe he had a row with his boss or his wife. See your work as that of a Geisha girl. The man must forget his everyday cares and worries. That is your objective.'

Sylvia suspected that Anita was a woman who also was quite experienced.

'It is profitable work,' she continued. 'Half of the fee, which you see in the catalogue, is for you. The other half is for the house. It's up to you, the more customers you get the more you earn.'

There was a general murmur of approval.

'But, what about income tax?' asked Laura, nervously. 'I don't want to jeopardise my social allowance.'

'The only thing you have to pay is VAT over your services and that is deducted by us,' answered Fred. 'Also, your identity is kept confidential. Is there anything else you wish to know?'

'Sex?' Marieke's eyes glanced from side to side as she asked the crucial question. 'If a client wants sex what must we do?'

'Are you crazy? Sex?' Anita spluttered the word out as if it was something disgraceful. 'Sex is against the rules. It is totally forbidden. If a client wants sex you must advise him to go somewhere else. This is a massage salon and you are masseuses not whores. The objective is to massage a man in such a way that he is kept aroused and is eventually satisfied without the need for the full treatment.'

She stretched her hand out and made erotic movements with her fingers. 'These are the tools of your trade. Learn to use them effectively and the men will keep coming back for more.'

As she listened Sylvia realised she was becoming aroused by the sensual nature of the discussion. She glanced down at her black stockings and high heels. This would be her working outfit from now on. She was beginning to look forward to the new challenge in her life. *Was she sexy enough? Was she sexier than Laura? Or Puck? Would she be attractive to the clients?*

She observed the other girls as they listened to Fred and Anita. Puck had a stoical expression on her face as she persisted with numerous detailed questions: 'What if the client offered her something to drink? In Amsterdam that was normal and even encouraged. Would she get a percentage?'

14

'And what if the client doesn't achieve an orgasm? Interrupted Marieke excitedly. 'If I do my best with my hands but it doesn't succeed must I try something else to satisfy him?'

Fred frowned and drew a deep breath. Sylvia could see that he was trying to restrain himself.

'Do you have a boy friend? He asked calmly.

Marieke nodded.

'Then you know how to satisfy him with your hands. Just imagine it's your boyfriend and you won't have a problem.'

'I've had plenty of boyfriends,' laughed Chantal. 'I can show you how it goes.' She picked up a red candle that was lying on the table, wrapped her long slender fingers around the top, and began to move them slowly up and down. There was complete silence in the room as everybody focussed on the demonstration. Anita stood with her mouth open. Fred looked amused and the man on the bar stood up to get a better look. Sylvia stared in astonishment as the black girl played with the candle like a phallus. She pressed it between her breasts and at the same time she moistened her lips with her tongue. She stroked it, squeezed it and played with the sensitive area under the tip. She covered the top with the palm of her hand and circled it with her finger tips moving them slowly up and down. On her face was a sensual look, as if she was alone in the room with her imaginary victim. She began to move her hands faster and faster, then with a sudden loud grunt she pushed down hard and stopped, to simulate an uncontrollable ejaculation.

'See, you just need a little practice? Chantal laughed, as she tossed the candle back on to the table.

Fred put his thumbs up in approval. 'Well done,' he said. 'I was beginning to wish I was a candle.'

Everybody was now completely relaxed and the place was quickly filled with chatter, laughter and activity as the girls began to explore the salon. Downstairs they tried out the showers, the sauna and the whirlpool. Upstairs in the massage rooms they were given instructions and advice by Anita.

Sylvia stayed sitting at the table to finish her coffee and to touch up her make-up. The mystery man at the bar was staring at her again. He picked up his glass, moved towards the table and took the seat next to her.

'We haven't been introduced yet. My name is Hans van der Terp. I am the owner of the building. Fred and Anita are responsible for the business, but as they are close friends of mine I like to pop in sometimes to see how things are going.

'Let's hope it becomes a big success,' Sylvia said, feeling slightly uncomfortable. 'Then all your efforts will be worth while.' She could feel the penetrating eyes of Jolanda who was sitting on the other side of the table. She had a stern looked on her face and, without saying a word, stood up collected the empty coffee cups and took them to the bar.

Sylvia was relieved when, once again, Anita called all the girls back to the table.

'Time flies,' she said. 'It is eleven-o-clock and we are now open for business. We must prepare ourselves for the first client.'

The girls returned to their seats and Fred moved behind the bar, turned on some background music, and poured himself a beer. Anita joined him and began fidgeting with the flower arrangements and filling some dishes with nuts.

Hans van der Terp went back to the bar, said something to Jolanda, then turned round and waved. 'Success everybody, it's time for us to leave.'

It was time for the first client to arrive. Nobody spoke a word. Sylvia felt her heart beating in anticipation. Chantal began tapping on the table with her finger nails until she noticed Puck looking annoyed. Marieke tried to arrange herself into a sexy posture. Laura moved her white coat higher to display more of her black stockings.

The minutes ticked by. Five minutes! Ten minutes! Thirty minutes! It seemed like hours. Anita looked concerned. 'You may put the television on ladies, if you are bored.'

Puck picked up the remote control and tried the various channels until she found the soap, Jerry Springer.

Laura smoked one cigarette after the other. A few times she looked at Sylvia and raised her eyebrows. Sylvia knew what she was thinking and shrugged her shoulders in response. Chantal was beginning to doze off and Marieke was fiddling with the rings dangling from her ears.

16

At last he arrived, an older, smartly dressed, distinguished looking man, with thick grey hair. As he approached the bar he looked a little uneasy as the battery of eyes focussed on him.

Fred reacted immediately, like a well trained professional he moved closer to put him at his ease. 'Hallo Sir! Please take a seat, this is our opening day and you are our first customer.' He extended his hand. 'I'm Fred, welcome to our salon. Would you like a coffee? It's on the house.' He moved the tray of nuts closer, 'Take as many as you like.'

'I'd love a coffee,' the man answered, taking off his coat and placing it on the stool next to him. 'I saw your advertisement in the local paper and thought I'd come along and check it out. It's a much nicer place than I expected, but I did have a problem finding a parking spot.'

Fred shrugged his shoulders in sympathy. 'When we were looking for a good location the estate agent showed us this place during the peak skiing vacation period when there were plenty of parking spaces available. Now it is more difficult. If you come here again you should try the parking area at the back of the building. It is intended for residents and most of the time there is space available. Also, we have a back door that opens directly on to the parking area.

While Fred prepared the coffee the man began to look through the leather covered booklet, occasionally looking towards the girls. Sylvia was sure he was staring at her. She shrank back into the settee and picked up a magazine. She felt her heart pounding and her cheeks colouring. '*Not me,*' she thought, '*I can't be the first.*' Then she realised that he was looking at each girl in turn. Puck instinctively straightened up and took a deep breath to accentuate her contours. The man looked again at the menu and asked Fred some questions. Fred turned and said something to Anita who smiled and came close to the girls. She leaned over the table and said quietly, 'Puck, the man at the bar would like you to join him.'

Puck smiled knowingly at the other girls as she stood up, went to the bar and sat next to the visitor.

'Puck,' said Fred enthusiastically. 'This gentleman would first like you to join him in the sauna and then he would like three quarters of an hour body-to-body. Can you take him downstairs, organise his shower and provide him with a bathrobe. The rest is up to you.'

Puck nodded. 'Please follow me,' she said, as she took his hand and led him to the stairs which were located behind the office.

'The old tart,' hissed Laura between her teeth. 'We have to look out for her. I know that type.'

Chantal laughed. 'It's the same everywhere. Don't worry; we will all get our turn.'

Chantal was right. It was still early in the day. After another half hour the next visitor arrived, and then the next. They began to trickle in steadily one after the other. Most of them had been intrigued by the advertising campaign in the local press. One or two, who lived nearby, had noticed the building renovations and were curious to find out what was happening in their neighbourhood.

Laura was the second to be chosen, by a small, not very attractive young man wearing glasses. He was rather shy and nervous. Sylvia watched intently as Laura introduced herself, sat next to him and began to explain the programs. She followed their movements as they went down to the changing room and saw them pass Puck and her client, clad in bath robes, on the way up to the massage rooms.

Sylvia's imagination began to take over. She began to fantasise about how Puck would treat her client. How she would instruct him to lie on the massage bed while she slid sensuously out of her white coat and slowly removed her underwear. How she would straddle him with her naked body and smother him in massage oil and how.......

'Sylvia! Sylvia! Didn't you hear me,' Fred was shaking her shoulder. 'There is a client at the bar who would like a one hour Tantra massage from you. Will you go and introduce yourself.'

Suddenly she was wide awake. She looked at Chantal in panic. 'What in heavens name is a Tantra?'

Chantal picked up the red candle and took Sylvia's hand. She moved her hand up and down and fingers round and round. 'Just take your time and don't finish him off too quickly. Make it last until his time is up.'

She went to the bar and gave the man her hand. 'Hello. I'm Sylvia.' She sat on the stool next to him, instinctively making a fast mental appraisal of her first client. He was quite good looking, in his mid thirties with dark brown hair, brown eyes and a well built body.

He smiled at her. 'Nice to meet you, my name is Theo, please join me in a glass of wine,' he said, giving a sign to Fred. 'Your boss has just been telling me that you are new to this sort of work and that I'm your first client.' He looked at her admiringly. 'So, I expect this will be an interesting experience for both of us.'

'Let's hope so.' Sylvia picked up her wine glass and took a sip. She found the man to be both sympathetic and exciting. An irrepressible warm and erotic feeling began to flow through her body. 'Would you like to try the Sauna first?'

'I'd love to try the sauna, but not this time thanks. My parking meter runs out in just over an hour.'

'In that case, why don't we take these with us,' she suggested, picking up the wine glasses. 'Just follow me, I'll show you where you can put your clothes and take a shower.'

When the man had finished his shower and put on his bath robe Sylvia led him upstairs. As they passed the reception room she noticed Chantal giving her the thumbs up.

As they walked through the door of the massage room they entered another world, a world of intimacy and sensuality. New world music was gently playing in the background and there was an aroma of scented massage oil. The dim, warm coloured lights gently illuminated the maroon and gold décor. On the ceiling was a large tinted mirror surrounded by tiny twinkling stars.

Without saying a word Sylvia took the man's bathrobe and waved her hand towards the massage table. As he moved into position, lying face downwards Sylvia realised she was now on her own, with a stranger, a handsome man, completely naked, waiting for some intimate massage treatment.

She carefully poured a little oil into her hands and began to spread it in gentle circular movements over his back. Then, remembering Marieke's demonstration, she moved her hands higher and began to massage his neck and shoulders with more pressure. He eased himself into a slightly more relaxed position, murmuring 'That's nice, keep going.' She continued with more enthusiasm, using more oil and pressing harder with her fingers and thumbs, massaging his back, along his spine, under his shoulder blades and down to his waist. She repeated the sequence two or three times. She began to sense the subtle interaction between her hands and the flesh beneath her. Discreetly she kicked off her high heels to improve her balance. To avoid arousing the man too quickly she passed over his buttocks and moved down to with his legs.

She started with his feet and, as she had read somewhere in a magazine, pressed gently under his toes and then scraped her nails softly along the sole of his foot. This caused an involuntary reaction as the man jerked his foot away. She moved slowly to his calves and then to his thighs. She spread her fingers widely to grip the firm flesh and continued with strong squeezing and circular movements. The man's eyes were closed and his body was completely relaxed. He did not speak and seemed to be in a trance.

She was beginning to enjoy herself as she teasingly moved her finger tops lightly over his shoulders and around his waist. For a few seconds she caressed gently between his thighs. The man groaned softly.

'Your first half hour is up,' she whispered sexily. 'It's time to turn over.'

'I was almost asleep.' he sighed, as he turned onto his back. He stretched his arm out stroked his fingers over her face. 'For a beginner you are doing an excellent job and you look good as well.' His eyes were roving over her figure approvingly. 'Are you sure you can't take this off?' He asked touching her white coat.

'Yes of course. Sorry, you have a one hour program, don't you?' She quickly unbuttoned and took off her coat, displaying a very sexy bra and string.

The man let out a soft whistle of approval. 'That's very nice. What a waste to keep such assets hidden. Does that have to stay on as well?' He was sitting up and trying to reach her bra straps. 'I would prefer to see you all of you.'

'Sorry, but for that you have to take another program.' She said, pushing him firmly back on to the massage table. 'Just relax; otherwise I can't massage you properly.'

'Okay, you are in charge,' he said, looking slightly resentful.

She ignored his mock resentment and began to massage his neck muscles and shoulders. She worked slowly round his chest and waist and gently squeezed his nipples. At the same time she could not resist glancing at his manhood further down. She was fascinated as she watched it gradually becoming larger. Eventually, unable to restrain herself, she ran her finger tips lightly and sensually over his chest and tummy and, almost by accident, over 'that strange thing.' It reacted immediately and moved

20

upwards into a vertical position, stiff and erect. Her curiosity was now fully aroused and she couldn't resist playing with it, running her fingers slowly up and down, and, round and round. The man groaned and opened his legs slightly. She understood the invitation and stroked her fingers lightly over the round objects that were now exposed.

Sylvia felt a warm glow flowing through her body. She felt excited at the reactions she was causing. Her basic instincts were taking over. Any inhibitions she might have had were vanishing quickly as she concentrated on maximising the sexual arousal of her victim.

She was fascinated at how much his organ had grown. It had increased to at least twenty centimetres long and was as stiff as a poker. She caressed it with both hands and began to move the outer skin slowly up and down. She began to experiment with her movements, trying different pressures and speeds, working first with one hand and then with two. Whenever he seemed to be getting close to a climax she stopped to allow him to calm down. Eventually his hour was almost up and, remembering the few occasions when she had finished off her boyfriend, she speeded up her movements. His body stiffened and he began to let out uncontrollable grunts and groans of pleasure. Suddenly white spurts of cream shot out over his stomach and over her hands. She continued with a few gentle squeezing movements until his orgasm had completely subsided.

'Did you enjoy that?' she laughed, as she handed him some tissues and helped him clean up.

'It was overwhelming,' he said, leaning up on one elbow to give her a kiss on the cheek. 'For a beginner you are learning fast.'

Sylvia smiled with relief, pleased that she had succeeded with her first client.

He eased himself off the table and put on his bath robe. 'I shall certainly come back soon,' he said, with a naughty grin on his face. 'Your body to body program sounds even more exciting. Then I can see all of your body. Now I just have time for another shower to remove all that oil that you used so generously.'

'I shall tell your boss that you have a natural talent,' he said, as he left the room.

She carefully washed her hands, then tidied up the room and the massage table, put her white coat and high heels back on, put the lights out and closed the door.

'*Mission accomplished,*' she thought, as she went down the stairs, still in a slight daze. She could sense the eyes of the other girls looking at her, trying to judge her reactions.

'How was it?' Chantal was unable to control her curiosity.

'No problem at all. In fact I quite enjoyed it,' she answered, putting on an air of confidence. 'But now I need a drink.'

Fred was already pouring her a cola when she sat at the bar. 'Well done,' he said, with that inscrutable, almost smug, look of satisfaction that only he could give. 'Your client has just left and he was very complimentary about your performance. He will almost certainly be back for another appointment soon.' For a few seconds there was an invisible bond of friendship between them. 'Do your best for me and I'll do my best for you,' he said encouragingly.

She finished her drink and rejoined the other girls. As she relaxed into a corner of the settee she began to reflect over the events that had just taken place, still feeling sexually aroused. She found the work exciting and could hardly believe that it could be so easy. Any doubts she had about her suitability for the work were fast disappearing. '*It's just a way of giving a man pleasure and relieving his pent up emotions,*' she persuaded herself. '*It's not doing anybody any harm; it's just a form of therapy treatment.*'

Chantal and Marieke were busy chatting about their past experiences. Their accents lacked refinement and they did not give the impression of being particularly intelligent, but they were cheerful and seemed to have had a wide range of experience. That is, if you believed everything they said. The coffee pot and several cups that were scattered around the table were quickly becoming a permanent feature.

Laura was sitting next to her quietly reading a magazine and smoking a cigarette.

'Where's Puck?' Sylvia asked. 'She can't still be busy with her first Client?

'No, of course not, he left over half an hour ago. She has almost finished with her second client. Older men seem to be her speciality. Look! They are just returning to the bar, now's your chance to see her in action.'

They watched surreptitiously, as Puck guided her client to the bar like an over attentive chaperone. He was even older than her first client and as he sat down she signalled Fred for some drinks and moved her stool closer. She began to talk to him in an over enthusiastic and flirtatious manner, like an old friend. As she laughed flatteringly at his comments her hand rested

22

on his arm and her thigh pressed closer to his. The man seemed to enjoy the attention and requested another round of drinks, including one for Fred and Anita. Eventually when he decided to leave, Puck helped him into his coat, took him to the door and gave him a farewell kiss on the cheek.

'You certainly know how to treat a client,' said Anita, as she returned to the bar. 'It's obvious that you have plenty of experience.'

'Well! I like them to leave with a happy feeling.' She answered proudly. 'Then they are more likely to come back.'

'That's something I forgot to do,' Sylvia blurted out. Feeling annoyed with herself.

'Oh, yes,' Laura was nodding her head. 'Always finish the job by taking them to the shower and escorting them back the bar.'

A few hours had passed, it was late afternoon and all the girls were getting hungry.

'Fred, what do we do for food?' asked Puck 'Do we have to go to a nearby cafe, or can we organise some take-away?'

'Don't worry,' said Fred. 'As it's your first day we will organise it for you.'

During the renovation work Fred and Anita had got used to ordering take-away and they had accumulated a collection of menus from the local restaurants.

'What do you prefer ladies? Pizza, Chinese, Hamburgers?'

After a lot of discussion they settled for Chinese, as it was easier to order a wide range of dishes and keep everybody happy.

When they had finished eating and the food had been cleared away Sylvia began to feel restless, she was still waiting for her second client. She must get used to this new routine; having to sit around for hours but always looking glamorous and seductive and ready to spring into action.

The other girls were more experienced. They kicked off their shoes put their legs up on the cushions and even dozed off, completely relaxed. But, whenever a customer walked in they awoke immediately and instinctively positioned themselves into their most provocative poses.

Sylvia picked out a magazine from the collection on the table and flicked half interested through the pages. Every time the door opened and a prospective client walked in she stiffened up and closely followed Fred's actions as he went through what was quickly becoming a standard routine. She observed how he would first offer the man a drink, then, after a few words would wave a hand towards the girls, at the same time trying to assess the man's preferences. He would then show the client the little brown book and explain the programs available and the prices. Some had obviously seen the advertisement and had only come out of curiosity. After getting a free drink, listening to Fred, and sizing up the girls, they would leave with a promise to return another day.

Then, at last, a handsome Italian looking young man walked in, hung his coat up by the door and went to the bar. His confident manner suggested that he was here for a purpose. He was welcomed by Fred and put through his promotion routine. Sylvia immediately sat up enthusiastically, shook her hair into place, placed one leg evocatively over the other and put a mysterious look on her face. Laura went through a similar routine and glanced with a seductive smile at the man. She saw the man say something to Fred who turned to look at the girls.

'Laura, would you like to come and join us?'

Laura stood up graciously, and with a superior smile, walked elegantly to the bar and introduced herself. After a few words she took the man by the hand and led him downstairs. Sylvia watched admiringly '*I can learn a few tricks from her,*' she thought.

Marieke, sitting nearby, let out a sigh of dismay. She was the only girl not to have had a client, and this was Laura's second. Sylvia also could not help feeling jealous as she heard the cheerful chattering downstairs and the sound of the whirlpool being turned on. Then a door closed and there was silence. She could not help visualising the man's reaction as Laura disrobed and her naked sexy figure joined him in the warm pulsing water.

'She is a blond, slender and attractive, that's why she gets chosen,' grunted Chantal. 'I'm black and rather large and that intimidates some men.'

'You are also beautiful, Chantal. There are plenty of men looking for something exotic and unusual,' said Puck reassuringly.

'Yes, but I live in a white land.' She laughed, showing her sparkling white teeth. 'In my own country I would have been married long ago with a rich man.'

'Why are you still here then?' murmured Marieke. 'That's what I'd like to know.'

Chantal ignored the naïve remark and kept silent. Sylvia frowned at Marieke for being so mean. '*Are squabbles beginning already?*' she thought.

Then she noticed a man sitting at the bar near the door, half hidden by one of the bouquets of flowers. He had entered unnoticed by Fred and the others. He was a rather thin, pleasant looking young man. He was smartly dressed in a suit, wearing a bright tie and glasses. She was sure he was looking directly at her. She pretended not to notice, but stood up and reached over the table to pick up a magazine, to show off her long legs and long hair. Fred had now seen the man and moved quickly into action. He signalled to Anita to provide a cup of coffee, while he gave the man a cigarette. He chatted to the man in a relaxed manner as he explained the options. He could be quite charming when necessary and always let the client take his time.

The other girls were now joining in the action, each trying in their own way surreptitiously to send the man a signal. 'If that guy looks at me again I'm going to wave,' whispered Chantal. 'Hurry up man, make your choice.'

Sylvia was getting nervous. *'Was he interested in her? Was that wink directed at her?'* She looked at Fred but saw no reaction. She smiled in his direction and, yes, this time it was a clear signal. He was looking directly at her and crooked his finger, beckoning her to join him.

'So, you got the message at last,' he said, as she approached the bar.

'Sorry, but I wasn't certain.' She replied, moving her stool closer to his.

He gave her his hand. 'My name is Martin. Would you like something to drink?'

'A seven up please. My name is Sylvia.'

Fred poured out her drink, frowning slightly at her and she realised that she was supposed to ask for something more expensive.

Martin smiled at her encouragingly while he opened the menu book and studied the options. 'A body-to-body for three quarters of an hour? Is that possible?' he asked, looking at Fred.

'Of course that's possible.' Fred looked at Sylvia. 'You had better use the room at the end of the corridor. It's the best for a body-to-body'

Sylvia felt herself blushing and her pulse rate speeding up. *Body-to-body with a complete stranger? Why must he choose this program? How could she escape?* She looked desperately at Fred, but he pretended not to notice.

'You look a little nervous. Is this your first body-to-body?' The man asked.

'Well, yes actually, but it's no problem. I can handle it.' She forced herself to put on a look of confidence.

'Don't worry, there is always a first time for everything and anyway you will be in charge. I will leave everything to you.' He stood up and nonchalantly threw some notes on the bar. 'I'd first like to take a shower. Can you take me to the changing room and provide me with a bathrobe and towel.'

As she led the way downstairs she realised she was trapped, she could no longer escape. She must now use her body to give a service to a man in return for payment.

While the man was in the shower she ran up to the upper floor to prepare the massage room. She had previously checked all the rooms and she knew that room at the end of the corridor was the most luxurious. It was also the one furthest away from any listening ears below. For her first client she had used a smaller room, provided with a massage table only. This room was larger and much more intimate. It was romantically furnished, with a large double four-poster bed framed in heavy velvet drapes. The bed was covered with a red satin sheet and matching cushions. Above the bed was suspended a large tinted mirror. In the corner a vase of flowers had been placed on a small round glass table, and next to it stood an ornate gold coloured chair. Small beams of light flickered in through the lamella blinds covering the windows and calming music was playing in the background. She closed the curtains over the window and lit some candles.

On the way back downstairs her panic feelings subsided and she even began to feel a little excited. 'What adventure had she now let herself in for?'

The man did not speak as she led him up to the massage room. Directly they entered the room he took off his bathrobe, threw it on the chair and laid down on the bed. Sylvia hesitated for a moment, unsure what to do next. The man on the bed waved his hands enthusiastically to show what was expected. Everything off! And fast!

'Not so fast,' she thought. She first dimmed the lights down lower, until only candle light illuminated the room. She then slowly took off her white coat and stood in a provocative pose. The man on the bed let out a gasp of approval. Slowly and sensually she took off her bra and, as modestly as possible, her string.

'Gorgeous,' he gasped, as she knelt on the bed. His hand stroking gently down her back.

She pushed his hand away. 'Turn over. Lay on your front,' she said in a firm voice. Her nervousness had completely disappeared and she was now in control. She picked up a bottle of massage oil from the table next to the bed and sprinkled some oil on his back. She began to massage him with her hands. After a few minutes she spread some oil over her breasts and carefully straddled his body with her legs and arms. She then lowered herself down and began to move her breasts lightly over his back. Her nipples were firm and erect and the man gave a groan of pleasure. She tried various positions, first massaging his shoulders and neck with her hands and then moving her breasts over his lower back and buttocks. The man

28

had a slender build and she took care not to put her full weight on him. She continued the treatment over his thighs and legs, varying from hard massaging with her hands to erotic movements with her body. When her arms became too tired from supporting her weight in such a horizontal position, she sat up and ran her fingernails lightly over his body from top to bottom. She was surprised as she felt his body tense up in excitement. She began to experiment, to see which techniques produced the most reaction. She was learning fast. As though by accident she let her hand move between his thighs and got an instant jerking response.

Realising she must keep things calm for a while; she moved to a sitting position on the side of the bed and leaned over to reach for the massage oil. This made the man curious. He turned on his side to look at her and could not resist extending his hand and touching her breasts and playing gently with her nipples. Although she enjoyed the erotic feeling she knew she must stick to the program.

'You may only turn round when I say so,' she said, pushing his hand away 'I am not yet ready.' Submissively he turned back on to his tummy without saying a word.

She was beginning to understand that erotic massage was a combination of relaxation and sexual arousal. Instinctively she knew that she must learn how to dominate her clients and to manipulate their sexual feelings. How to provoke an arousal? How to calm things down? How to achieve the final climax? All within the time span of the selected program. Only she could decide what was and what wasn't allowed.

She continued with her massaging routine, occasionally looking at the small clock hanging discretely in a corner of the room. Her client gradually calmed down and was almost asleep. When the clock eventually indicated half time, she rolled off his body to the side of the bed. 'Okay! You can turn over now.'

He turned over obediently. His eyes now wide open, looking admiringly at her figure and waiting expectantly for her next move. Once again she straddled his body, sitting on his thighs, taking care not to make contact with his penis which was now rapidly growing in size. She sprinkled his chest with oil and began the second part of her massage routine. She began with her hands, massaging his shoulders, his arms and his chest and tummy. She then bent lower and moved her breasts over the upper part of his body. Immediately she felt the reaction as something under her stiffened and pressed into her tummy.

'You're driving me crazy,' he grunted 'When are you going grab that thing and finish it off?'

'I'm in charge, remember? You want to get your money's worth, don't you?

The clock was telling her that only ten minutes time was left. She moved her body lower and let her breasts brush softly over his penis. The man gasped uncontrollably. She sat up straight and put her hand gently round it and began fondling it.. She could sense the power in her fingers. Her victim was now completely at her mercy. At first she moved her hands slowly up and down, then faster and faster. She tried out sensual finger movements and played with the surrounding skin and the exposed tip. When she thought he was close to a climax she stopped for a few seconds, then began slowly again, building up to another climax. She played in a teasing, slightly sadistic manner, determined to delay his orgasm as long as possible.

At last she realised he was loosing control. His body was rigid. There was no stopping now. She moved her hands faster and faster until, suddenly, she could sense his climax beginning. She slowed down her hand movements, pushed downwards and squeezed gently, watching in fascination as the uncontrollable pulses of white creamy substance surged out and flew through the air, almost reaching his chin.

He slumped back into the bed temporarily exhausted. While he was recovering she took some tissues from the box standing on the table next to the bed and wiped his body clean. Then she lay on her side next to him, put an arm over his waist and teased his feet with her toes. She noticed him looking at their reflection in the mirror above them.

After a few minutes he sat up and gave her a kiss on the cheek. 'That was fantastic; you have a natural talent and you seem to enjoy it yourself.' He stood up and put on his bathrobe. 'Now I must hurry. I must shower and get to my car before the traffic warden arrives.'

Sylvia eased back into the softness of the bed to relax for a few minutes and to recover from her exertions. The picture reflected in the mirror above drew her attention; it was like a voyeuristic painting by Goya, a white sensual female body with long dark hair reclining on a background of sumptuous colours. It was surreal. Was this really her? Suddenly she felt rather insecure and vulnerable. She jumped off the bed, wrapped herself in a bathrobe, grabbed her clothes and rushed downstairs to take a shower.

She reached the shower room just as her client was leaving. He looked quite refreshed and smiled cheerfully. 'I will be back to see you again soon. Goodbye.'

When she had showered, dressed and fixed her make-up she returned to the lounge. Marieke was sitting alone watching the television. She looked unhappy, as she was still the only one not to have been chosen. She brightened up when Sylvia sat next to her. 'Your client has just left. He looked like a nice young guy,' she said, rather enviously. 'He had a quick drink and chat with Fred before he left. He seemed to be very satisfied.'

'Oh! I've done it again,' she said, seeing Fred's frowning face behind the bar. 'I must remember to escort the client to the door when he leaves.' She stood up and went to the bar.

'Don't forget,' he said, as she approached. 'After a massage, your work isn't finished. You must learn to arrange your routine so that you have time for a few words with your client before he leaves. And when he does leave, you should see him to the door. This time he was in a hurry and you were still busy. Anyway, you did well. He was very satisfied and even left you a tip, which I will give you later.'

'Don't worry about it,' said Marieke, as Sylvia sat next to her again. 'It's not that important. It's only a formality. If they are satisfied and have enough time they will usually invite you to join them at the bar for a drink and a cosy chat. Then you have a good chance to soften them up for their next visit.'

She continued philosophically. 'When men come to these places they are just like naughty children, breaking the rules and doing something forbidden. After they have achieved their objective they quickly lose interest.'

Sylvia nodded and relaxed back into the comfort of the settee. She began to think back over the last few days. Things had changed so fast. She felt both elated and confused at the same time. Had she done the right thing? When she decided to leave her previous job the personnel manager had been reluctant to let her go. He had tried to persuade her that it was a steady job with reasonable long term prospects. But, she had found the work so frustrating. After a lot of hard selling on the telephone, you were lucky if one person per day showed any interest in insurance. Eventually, out of curiosity, she had begun to scan through the work ads and, as a result, here she was, sitting in these exotic surroundings, competing with a bunch of sexy ladies trying to sell their attributes to horny men. It wasn't real sex and maybe it was harmless, but it wasn't considered normal in society.

It was fortunate, she thought, that in her personal life, outside the salon, nobody needed to know what she was up to. She could easily keep up the pretence that she was still working at the insurance office, and fortunately her work in the salon would be kept confidential.

Puck had given her a useful tip. 'You must organise a separate mobile telephone which you can use exclusively for business calls. Then you can receive calls or messages directly from any of your clients wishing to make an appointment.'

Even so, she still couldn't help feeling a bit insecure. She must live a life of deception. She visualised the stern look of her father when he disapproved of something. He must never find out what she was up to.

Once again she looked around bemused at her new surroundings. The colourful Buddha's with their tranquil expressions, the tinted mirrors giving the illusion of more space, the ornate glass coffee table now covered with finger prints, the dark red carpets and drapes and the soft background music. It was almost like a bordello. *'What will this world teach her?*

She looked at the clock; it was nearly closing time. Fred had disappeared into his office to work out their payments. The other girls had all returned. They were beginning to look tired. The excitement from all their activities and exertions had taking their toll.

At last! Anita stood up, looking at her watch. 'Well done ladies' she said in a cheerful voice. 'It's been a very successful day, thanks to your efforts. Now it's time for us all to go home. You can change back to your normal clothes and leave your working outfits in your lockers downstairs. Fred will give you your payments before you leave.'

One by one they went into the office to collect their money. Sylvia felt slightly disappointed, having had only two clients, but was pleased with the generous tip from her last customer. 'Don't worry,' said Fred. 'It's only the first day. Our clientele should steadily increase. Your objective is to build up regular clients that come back exclusively for you.'

Only Laura was very satisfied. She had been the top performer. Puck had also made a good start, although she seemed to attract the older clients. Marieke had to leave with nothing.

*S*ylvia's second day in Body Line started with more promise. She had arrived a few minutes early and as she walked through the door and her eyes had adjusted to the light she saw two customers already sitting at the bar. One of them was a cheerful looking, sturdily built youngish man with curly brown hair. He was neatly dressed in a woollen pullover and jeans. He was talking to Fred and drinking a cup of coffee. The other man, sitting a few stools further along the bar, was wearing a brightly coloured shirt and jeans. He was also drinking coffee and reading the morning newspaper. Anita, who was busy in the background rearranging some cushions, paused to give her a wave.

Fred looked relieved when he saw her. 'Good morning Sylvia, you are the first girl to arrive,' he said, glancing at the clock. 'By coincidence we were just talking about you. This young man is looking for an attractive and entertaining young lady, preferably with a slender figure and I think you are the obvious choice. Why don't you sit down and introduce yourself.'

Sylvia was taken by surprise; she had no time to think. She hung her jacket by the door, dropped her bag in the corner and took the stool next to the man.

He put down his cup. 'My name is Peter, pleased to meet you.'

'I'm Sylvia,' she said, shaking his hand in as professional manner as possible. She noticed his eyes quickly roving over figure. 'Have you chosen a program yet?'

'More or less, but I was waiting to see if what Fred said about you was true.'

'This gentleman would like to begin with a sauna, followed by a whirlpool and finally a body-to-body massage,' interrupted Fred hastily; worried that he might change to a shorter program. 'Why don't you go and change your clothes while he finishes his drink? The sauna is already on but you must prepare the whirlpool. It' takes five minutes to fill up.'

'That's fine with me.' The man was smiling cheerfully at her. 'I'm quite happy to wait for such a charming young lady. Let me know when you are ready.'

Sylvia stood up, picked up her bag and went downstairs. She was pleased to have been chosen so quickly, but also felt slightly indignant. She had been pushed into something without having first been given a choice.

Fred could have been more polite and taken her to one side to ask her if she was interested.

She changed into her sexy underwear and high heels and, before putting on her white coat, checked her appearance in the full length mirror next to the lockers. She was very satisfied with what she saw. Her irritation with Fed had disappeared and she now felt relaxed and confident. Her experiences yesterday had taught her a lot. She knew what to expect and was even looking forward to trying out her knew found talents on her next victim.

As she went to the whirlpool room she could hear the noise upstairs as the other girls arrived. She turned on the taps of the whirlpool and adjusted the temperature of the water. While the bath was filling she checked out the room. The walls and the floor were covered with white tiles, giving a clean and sterile impression. She quickly hid away a mop and a bottle of cleaning liquid, which had been provided for cleaning up after use of the whirlpool, and turned down the lights to give a more intimate atmosphere. When the bath was full she turned off the taps and went back upstairs, passing Laura on the way.

'Hello Sylvia!' she said, cheerfully. 'You're off to an early start, and with quite a sexy young guy. I've been chosen by the other guy, the one in the bright shirt.'

She waved to Puck and Chantal who were sitting on the settee drinking coffee. They seemed to be in no hurry to change into their working outfits. Marieke had just arrived, again complaining about the transport.

Her client, Peter, had finished his drink and stood up enthusiastically as she approached. She led the way downstairs to the changing room and showed him a locker for his clothes, gave him a towel and a bathrobe, and showed him how to operate the shower.

'I'll be back in five minutes,' she said, as she once again ran up the stairs. She collapsed on the seat next to Puck.

'At last I've got time for a coffee,' she gasped. 'Before he finishes his shower,'

'Normally for a program beginning with a sauna it is not necessary to shower first,' said Puck curtly, as though it was obvious. 'After the sauna he must shower again.'

'So what?' reacted Sylvia coolly. 'This way I can be certain that he is clean.'

34

Marieke overheard her remark and laughed spontaneously. 'For some men two showers are not enough,' she said in a loud voice.

'Some men need ten showers,' Chantal joined in, laughing. 'Yesterday I had a guy who was a bit overpowering. When I asked him when had last had a bath he couldn't remember. All he did was work, eat and sleep.'

'Maybe they should all pass a smell test before we let them get near us,' giggled Marieke. 'We could train a little sniffer dog, like they use at the airports. One woof for good, two woofs for bad.'

The girls were almost falling off their seats with laughter.

'Ladies!' Fred's loud sharp voice cut through the air. 'Such behaviour is out of place in this salon. I try to present you as ladies and expect you to behave with a little more decorum.'

It was suddenly silent. Marieke and Chantal exchanged rebellious looks. For an instant they were mutual friends. As Fred turned his back Chantal stuck up her long brown middle finger. 'Woof, woof,' she spluttered softly.

Marieke nearly choked, trying to muffle her laughter. Fred pretended to ignore their reactions. Puck kept herself aloof and frowned at all the commotion.

Sylvia returned downstairs, undressed and wrapped herself in a large bath towel just as her client finished his shower. As they entered the sauna she checked the temperature setting. Her client was obviously an experienced sauna goer, as he immediately spread his towel on the top bench and clambered into place. He purposely lay on his side so that he could watch her as she spread her towel and tried to lie as elegantly as possibly on the lowest level.

It took several minutes for her to get used to the high temperature and humidity. For a while it was quiet, except for an occasional sigh of contentment emanating from above. Then, as if by accident, an arm dropped down slowly next to her and fingers began to brush gently over the side of her sweating body. She did not resist and even felt a tingle of excitement.

'What sort of work were you doing before you came here?' He asked, as a way of starting a conversation. 'Fred told me that you have been rather enterprising.' As he spoke he moved down to her level and made himself comfortable on the bench next to her.

'Well, at school I did secretarial training, so my first job was in an office. My last job was in an insurance office. Before that I worked, for two years as the Dutch representative for a large English company renting out holiday homes in the south of France and in Spain. Sometimes I went on field trips with the boss, to check out new options.'

'Holiday homes? He looked at her admiringly. 'That must have been interesting. Why did you stop?'

Unfortunately changes in the currency exchange rates made it uneconomical and my boss had to give up the business.'

'So why are you working in a place like this?'

'Mainly because I wanted to try something different and to meet more people.'

In an attempt to distract the man from further personal questions she stroked her hand teasingly over his legs and toes. He reacted immediately by sitting up and moving closer to her. He casually put his hand on her thigh. She did not resist. She was beginning to find the man interesting. He was both sympathetic and arousing.

'And what do you do for a living.'

'Houses,' he answered. 'Buying and selling'.

'So, you are an Estate Agent?

'Not really, I buy houses that need renovation, upgrade them and put them back on the market.'

'At a good profit I suppose?' Sylvia began to find the conversation interesting. She moved into a sitting position next to him and put her hand on his knee.

'In most cases, he answered. 'But, it is not as easy as it sounds. It is a lot of hard work and it's difficult to keep the costs under control. Sometimes we even make a loss. But that's life. It's swings and roundabouts, sometimes you win and sometimes you lose. 'It's the same with you ladies, isn't it?' He looked at her with a cheeky smile; displaying brilliant white teeth against a sun tanned face. At the same time he put his arm round her shoulder and moved closer to her. She realised that he would prefer to change the subject.

'Hmm!' she murmured. 'Is that the reason you come to massage salons?'

'Naturally, it's a great way to relax, and, if you're lucky, to have some harmless fun with an attractive young lady. In these places you don't have to be worried about being ripped off with expensive, second rate champagne, almost before you have taken your coat off.'

'So, you visit sex clubs?' she asked, nervously.

36

'I don't like those places, but sometimes it's necessary to entertain business contacts. Personally I never make use of those ladies services.

Sylvia felt relieved, as during the conversation his other hand had moved slowly between her legs.

After a few minutes of erotic fondling he could no longer contain himself. He took her hand and moved it onto, what had now become a stiff erection. He leaned back and began to breathe heavily as she played with it gently with her fingers.

She realised that things were moving a bit too fast. She remembered that once a man has been finished off he can quickly lose interest.

'It's getting too hot for me here,' she said, giving a little squeeze with her hand. 'I think it's time to we moved to the whirlpool.'

The man covered himself discretely with his towel as he followed her into the dimly lit whirlpool room. She closed the door, checked the water temperature, turned on the water jets and sprinkled some aromatic oil over the water. Then she evocatively dropped her own towel and pulled his towel out of his hand. For a moment they stood admiring each others bodies.

'After you,' she said.

He stepped into the bath and stretched his body out under the warm pulsing water. He was looking at her with half closed eyes as she glided in next to him.

He pulled her closer. 'This is exciting. Why don't you show me what you are capable of?'

She moved into a sitting position on top of his legs and began to massage his neck and shoulders. She took her time and could not help admiring his athletic build as she ran her fingers teasingly over his chest and tummy. She could tell from his heavy breathing that he was getting sexually aroused. His penis was large and as stiff as an iron rod. Her breasts were now displayed in a provocative and vulnerable position and he could not resist fondling them with both hands. She was enjoying the attention and after a while moved into a lying position sliding slowly and sensually over his body, moving higher then lower. His hands instinctively moved over her back, pressing her closer. It was becoming intensely intimate.

After a few minutes she rolled to one side and sat up. 'I think we should calm down a little. I was almost losing control, and anyway, we still have to go upstairs for the last part of your program.'

37

'I was having such a good time I almost forgot that there was more to come.' He sat up, bent her head towards him and kissed her on the mouth.

They got out of the whirlpool, helped each other to dry off, then put on their bathrobes. Sylvia turned off the whirlpool and led the way up to her favourite massage room, the one at the end of the corridor.

'We still have twenty minutes to go,' she said with a smile. 'You had better lie on your tummy and relax, while I give you a normal massage.'

She sprinkled some oil over his back and began her massaging routine. But, he was too aroused and impatient, and after several minutes turned round.

'I can't wait any longer,' he said, moving her hand towards his penis which was still hard and erect.

She, was now used to the routine and began slowly, caressing it gently with her hands, varying her movements, fast and slow, up and down, and round and round. When she could sense from his body movements that he was losing control, she decided, this time, to try something new. She moved underneath him, pulled him on top of her and played hard with his penis until he was almost climaxing. She then sprinkled some oil on her breasts and guided it between them, squeezing her breasts together. He reacted instinctively, closing his eyes and thrusting in and out as though he was inside her pussy. It was obviously a new experience for him also, and after a few minutes of energetic movements he let out a gasp of pleasure as he ejaculated several spurts of warm soft liquid on to her breasts and chin.

They collapsed in each others arms and relaxed for a few minutes, while he helped her clean up with some tissues.

'That was sensational. You've got the perfect tits for that sort of treatment,' he murmured, playfully fondling them..

He looked at the clock, then sat up and turned her gently but firmly, face downwards, on the bed and moved his body above hers.

'I still have ten minutes left on my program. So, now it's your turn,' he said, pouring some oil into his hands. 'Just relax,'

He started with her neck and worked slowly down her body, her shoulders, her arms, her back, her waist, her legs. She had never been massaged before. It was very sensual experience. His hands were soft and tender and gradually she almost drifted into a trance like sleep.

'Time to turn round,' he said, giving her a little slap on her bottom.

She was immediately wide awake and as she turned she realised that she was in vulnerable position, she could easily lose control. She shut her eyes and instinctively kept her legs pressed together. As his hands touched her she felt an erotic thrill pass through her body.

He began to massage her again, starting with her neck and shoulders. As she didn't resist, he asked, 'Shall I go further?

'Don't stop,' she murmured.

He continued very gently with her breasts and tummy, and then moved to her legs. He lifted her legs one by one and massaged her calves and her thighs. He began to kiss her feet and moved his lips slowly along her legs. She could not resist as he eased her legs apart and moved his head between them. His tongue felt warm and vibrant. This was a new and irresistible feeling. She was losing control. She felt his fingers entering her and was soon lost in an overwhelming erotic sensation. If he had still been in a condition to take advantage of her she probably would not have resisted. But fortunately his peak had passed and their time had run out.

After they had finished showering he invited her to join him at the bar, where she had a glass of wine and he had a beer.

Now she was back at her usual place, sitting next to Laura and Chantal. Back to reality, but still unable to stop fantasising about her experience and dreaming of his next visit.

Laura sensed that she had behaved a bit naively and needed some advice 'Calm down Sylvia,' she said, putting her arm round her shoulder. 'You have obviously had a good time, but you mustn't forget rule number one. Never get romantically involved with a client. In their excitement here they will treat you like a queen, but once they are back outside in the real world they are more interested in their next meal.'

She nodded, pretending to agree, but in her heart she knew that this man was different. He was sincere, he had real feelings for her and she was sure that he would soon be back.

The rest of her day passed in a haze of confused emotions. After such an intense experience, combined with a little too much wine, she found it difficult to concentrate. She was not motivated to compete with the other girls and sat quietly in a corner of the settee. But, she was still chosen three times, twice for half hour basic massages and once for a one hour body-to-body. Apparently some clients were attracted by her demure composure.

*A*fter a good nights sleep, Sylvia's emotions had calmed down. She was now walking briskly along the familiar route to the salon feeling happy and looking forward to another day's work. But she still couldn't help thinking about the events of yesterday. She tried to convince herself that she had been overwhelmed by circumstances. She had never had such an erotic experience before and she must learn to separate physical satisfaction from genuine romantic feelings. Even so, she was sure that he would be back. Was Laura right or wrong?

Fred had also been concerned about her and, at the end of the day, had called her into his office to warn her about the problems of emotional attachments to clients.

As she stepped through the door she waved to Fred standing in his usual place behind the bar. Then her heart missed a beat. Who was that he was speaking to? She recognised his black curly hair. It was Peter! He was back, already sitting at the bar, waiting for her.

'Peter!' she gasped excitedly. 'What are you doing here so early?'

Any doubts she might have had vanished immediately, and she rushed to sit next to him.

'Well, I have half an hour to spare, and as we had such a marvellous time yesterday I thought I would stop in again for some more fun.' He put his arm round her shoulder. 'How about a quick body-to-body?'

'Oh!' Suddenly she felt disappointed. 'Only half an hour?'

'Time,' he sighed, avoiding her gaze. 'Unfortunately there is only twenty four hours in a day and I have so many other things to do.'

'O.K. then!' She jumped up abruptly, 'I shall organise your shower and wait up here until you are ready.'

When she returned Fred handed her a cola. He had a slightly cynical smile on his face and a look in his eyes that said, '*I told you so.*'

As she sat down she heard Chantal complaining loudly.

'Body-to-body,' that's what they all want in the end. Body-to-body, that's what I want. I haven't had anything yet Fred. The next client must be for me.'

'You should hold your mouth,' hissed Fred, as though stung by a wasp. 'If it doesn't suit you here you can go back to where you came from. I'm doing my best to build up a business, and I don't need all this complaining on my head. If you tried to look a little friendlier, then maybe you would be chosen more often.'

'Bah!' Her big dark eyes looked indignant. 'You call this a business,' she mumbled. 'A few clients a day, if you're lucky.'

She grabbed the remote control from the table and increased the volume on the TV. Fred immediately stepped closer, took the control out of her hand and reduced it back down.

Sylvia saw her client returning from his shower and quickly guided him upstairs to the massage room.

'The atmosphere seems to be a bit tense here today,' he said, as he manoeuvred himself onto the massage table. 'I can always sense when people are arguing.'

'There is nothing serious happening,' answered Sylvia, 'only the normal friction when people are boxed up together for hours. That can happen anywhere.'

'I suppose so. But, I must say, that dark girl does have some fire in her,' he said unexpectedly, lifting himself up on his elbows. 'I've never had a dark girl. Shall we ask her to join us?'

Sylvia could hardly believe what she had just heard.

'You have chosen a program with me,' her voice was suddenly cool and resentful. It was as though she was talking to a different man. Not the man she had dreamed about.

'Sorry,' he mumbled. 'There's no need to be so sensitive.' He turned on to his stomach and kept quiet for the rest of the half hour.

The spark had been extinguished and she went through her massage routine with only the pretence of enthusiasm.

Surprisingly, the tension between them did not diminish his arousal and she was amazed at his powerful climax when she finished him off. The thought of an angry lady giving him sexual satisfaction seemed to give him a perverse kick.

'Well! That was an unusual experience,' he said, as put on his bath robe and left the massage room. 'And who knows? Maybe I will be back for more.'

'*Not with me,*' she thought.

Feeling both disappointed and angry, she took her time tidying up the room, in the hope that he would have left before she returned downstairs.

She threw the tissues in the waste bin, straightened the bed covers and spread out a clean towel.

As she put on her high heels and bath robe she saw her reflection in a mirror. '*Not bad,*' she reassured herself. '*I don't need to get involved with an insincere guy like that, not with my assets.*'

As part of her duties she went directly down to the changing room and cleaned up the shower used by her client. Fortunately he was already gone.

She returned to the bar to calm down.

'Your client left in a hurry,' said Fred, frowning, 'And, I doubt if we will see him again. I hope you learned a lesson from that little escapade.'

'Don't worry, I realise I was a bit foolish.' she answered sheepishly. 'But I am over it now and I never want to hear the name Peter again.'

'There has also been another development,' said Fred. 'Marieke has left. It's a pity, but apparently she did not feel at home here. She was hardly ever chosen so she has decided to go back to SM.'

Anita, who was busy arranging a bouquet of flowers at the end of the bar, joined in. 'I'm not surprised, she wasn't really glamorous enough to interest the customers. Fortunately we still have enough girls.'

'Where are they all,' asked Sylvia, suddenly noticing they were all missing.

'They are all busy at the moment. Chantal is up stairs for a body-to-body, Laura is busy with a client in the sauna and Puck is downstairs with one of her elderly admirers.'

They could hear the commanding voice of Puck below in the changing room, giving instructions to her client.

Anita listened with admiration. 'She has certainly got the right touch. It reminds me of my past.'

'Have you also worked as a masseuse?' Sylvia, could not contain her curiosity. She had suspected that Anita had been hiding something.

'Well, yes, a few years ago.' She glanced at Fred, in case he disapproved. 'I was younger then of course and a free agent. But, I must say I was quite successful. That is partly the reason we took on this business.'

She finished arranging the flowers and picked up the accompanying card. She let out a sudden cry of joy.

'Jamiel? Fred, it's from Jamiel. He has sent us these flowers. And, he has added a note saying that he will be along to see us this evening.'

Fred had a beaming smile. It was fascinating to see such a change in his usually expressionless face. Apparently Jamiel was an old family friend. There was a sudden bustle of activity, the bar was cleaned and polished, fresh nuts were set out and the cooler was stocked up with beer.

Sylvia helped, clearing up the coffee cups and litter from the coffee table. She smiled at Chantal who was now looking cheerful. She had just finished an hour program with an Arab looking man. He apparently appreciated her treatment as he had even extended his program for an extra half hour.

Puck was recovering from a tiring program trying to satisfy the demands of her elderly client. She began chattering non-stop to Anita. 'Even when you've finished with their massage you still can't escape,' she complained. 'First they take ages to shower and dress. Then they are in no hurry to go home. They are probably lonely and expect you to give them constant attention while they sit down to recover and have two or three coffees and a bowl of nuts.'

Anita nodded occasionally, in a show of sympathy. When she caught Sylvia's eye she gave her a little frown as a signal to keep their little secret.

During the rest of the afternoon several clients had turned up and all the girls had been occupied. Sylvia had had two basic massage programs. Both clients had been pleasant business men who were easily satisfied, and she had found the work relaxing and fun. She had forgotten all about her emotional upset during the morning.

It was now the quiet period between five and seven-o-clock. It was the time for the girls to relax and to watch television.

Sylvia happened to be standing alone behind the bar pouring herself a glass of water, when the door opened and a rather unobtrusive middle aged man, carrying a brief case, walked in. She instinctively straightened up and put on a welcoming smile, assuming he was a potential customer. He was smartly dressed, had a neat hairstyle that tried to make the most of what little hair was remaining, and light grey eyes.

'I'm here to see your boss' he said, taking a business card out of his top pocket. 'Give this to him, he should be expecting me.'

Sylvia couldn't resist glancing at the card as she went to the office. *Gerard van Dijk, Finance and Pension Consultant,* she read.

Fred took the card and immediately rushed out of the office.

'Mr van Dijk, I was expecting you.' He smiled broadly, shook his hand and guided him to his office. On the way he turned to Sylvia. 'Would you mind making some coffee for my old friend? And please knock on the door when you are ready,' he said in a rather commanding voice.

As they entered the office she heard Fred saying, rather apologetically, 'We are expecting some new office furniture later this week.' Then the door marked 'Private' closed firmly behind them.

'*That is certainly someone he is trying to impress*' Thought Sylvia.

She put some water and coffee in the machine and turned it on. As she bent down to get some milk out of the cooler she suddenly noticed an overpowering perfume wafting through the air and she heard the rattle of cups and saucers. Puck had suddenly appeared and, without being asked, was busy arranging the coffee cups, saucers and sugar bowl on a tray.

'Nice of you to help,' snapped Sylvia. 'If you are so keen, you can finish the job yourself.' She plonked the milk carton on the bar and went to sit down on the settee next to Laura.

'What a meddler!' she hissed between her teeth. 'She thinks she can do everything better.'

'I know what you mean,' answered Laura reassuringly. 'But don't get upset. 'She won't last long.'

'What do you mean?'

'I know her type. Eventually she will put her foot in it.'

Sylvia couldn't help admiring Laura's relaxed and self assured manner. She eased back into the settee and pretended to read a magazine while she secretly observed her rival. Although in her mid thirties she was, so far, the salon's top performer. She had some sort of magnetic attraction for most men. She was both sophisticated and sexy at the same time. Her hair was golden blond and her blue eyes were accentuated by her sun-browned face. She knew how to dress and always wore coordinated outfits. Her green bra and matching pants shone through her semi-transparent white jacket. She had a slender figure and her long shapely legs were clad in shiny green high heel shoes. Sylvia was becoming curious about her previous experiences. Had she been married? Had she had many boyfriends?

Suddenly Laura leaned closer to her. 'Aren't you curious about this guy Jamiel? Look at how nervous Anita is. She can't stop fussing with her make-up.'

Sylvia put down her magazine and unobtrusively turned to look at the small Indonesian looking woman. She was sitting on a bar stool with a make-up case and mirror in front of her. She was busy back combing her hair and arranging it in a high bouffant. She then squinted into the mirror whilst she drew an eyeliner pen under her eyes and pouted her lips whilst she adjusted her lipstick; lastly she rubbed some rouge on her cheeks

'Ready for battle,' whispered Laura. 'That must be more than a casual friendship.'

At last, Fred and his mysterious visitor came out of the office. The man politely shook Anita's hand on his way out. Fred patted him on the back. 'I'll be in touch soon,' he said, opening the door. As he returned, he beckoned to Anita to join him in the office.

Sylvia picked up the remote control. It was past six o-clock and time to find a comedy program. For this work you needed much patience as there were many periods of boredom. To pass the time she mentally calculated her income and was satisfied. It was more than she would have earned in an office or shop and maybe she would earn some more this evening. However, she still felt some uncertainties about the work. Although she was enjoying herself she realised that it was not a long term career and she decided that in future she would bring some study books with her. For a start she would try to finish the English language course she had so eagerly started over a year ago.

The other girls were all relaxing. Chantal was dozing off as usual and Laura seemed to be miles away absorbed in her thoughts. Fred and Anita were still in the office.

Suddenly the peace was shattered. A loud bell sounded.

Chantal woke with a shock. 'Is that an alarm? Is there a fire?'

'Calm down,' said Puck, standing up. 'It's only the bell for the rear entrance. Luckily it's not used very often.'

'It's loud enough for the whole street to hear,' complained Chantal.

The massage salon is situated in a row of shops and offices on the street level of a large building. Above the street level are three floors of apartments. The back of the building faces a courtyard surrounded by similar apartments. The courtyard is used as a car park by the occupants of the apartments and the exit is via a short, narrow alleyway which opens out on to a busy shopping street.

Sylvia had discovered the shopping street on her second day. She had not taken any food with her and, when Fred and Anita were busy in the office, had quickly sneaked out the back door, with a coat over her working outfit, to find a baker for a sandwich.

They all turned in curiosity as Puck released the lock and opened the door.

A young, good looking, Indonesian man, wearing a brightly coloured batik shirt entered. He was carrying a large tray, covered in silver foil, which was giving off a delicious, appetising aroma.

'For the ladies of Body Line,' he announced in a loud voice and at the same time making a dramatic sweep with his free hand. 'I'm Roy,' he said removing the silver foil to display a variety of Indonesian delicacies. 'I have a restaurant and a take-away service just round the corner and hope to be of service to you. I can always give you a special price,' as he spoke his eyes looked intriguingly at the girls.

He put the tray on the coffee table. 'This is a typical Indonesian rice table. Help yourselves. This time it's on me.'

He waved to Anita. 'Hallo Anita. Is Fred here somewhere?'

At the same time the door of the office swung open and Fred came out smiling. He welcomed Roy as a long lost friend and took him to the bar for a cold beer.

It was perfect timing. All the girls had been getting hungry and they pounced on the dishes without ceremony. Sylvia was a little dubious at first as she was not familiar with oriental food. She found it tasty but spicy.

Anita joined them. 'This is traditional Indonesian food,' she explained. 'Fred and I eat it all the time. When I get time I cook it myself, but it takes a lot of time, so we usually get some take-away, from Roy. We have known him since Fred worked as a croupier in a nearby casino.'

'What does a rice table mean?' asked Sylvia.

Anita's eyes lit up. She was happy to explain. 'In Indonesia everybody eats rice at least twice a day. For a family meal a large bowl of rice is placed in the centre of the table and is surrounded by a variety of special dishes. These dishes can be just three or four, for a routine family lunch or dinner, but can exceed a hundred for a large feast or ceremony. Each person has a small bowl, a spoon and a fork, and helps him or herself first to a small portion of rice and then to one the special dishes. This is repeated until they have tried as many dishes as they fancy.'

'What are the dishes made from? Asked Laura, waving her hand in front of her mouth. 'They are quite spicy.'

'Well,' continued Anita, enthusiastically, 'they are not all spicy. It's a matter of trying them out. They can be made from almost anything, including; meat, chicken, fish, vegetables, nuts and fruit. They can be spicy, sweet or sour, or a combination of flavours.'

After the meal the quiet period continued and, to pass the time, Sylvia asked Fred if she could use the sauna.

He was still in deep conversation with Roy and waved his hand in such a manner as to indicate; 'Do as you please, but don't bother me.'

Downstairs it was quiet and peaceful. She put her clothes in her locker and grabbed a bath towel. When she entered the sauna the heat nearly overwhelmed her. She adjusted the setting of the temperature controller and made herself comfortable on the lowest level bench. Now was her chance to unwind. For the past few weeks her life had been like a roller coaster or a fast moving film. She closed her eyes and tried to sink into a meditative state, focussing only on the simple pleasures of life. Her fantasies took over and she closed her eyes.

Knock! Knock!

She opened her eyes with a shock. She could see a shadowy figure outlined through the condensation on the glass door. She quickly covered herself with her towel as an elderly grey haired man opened the door.

'Sorry to disturb you. Fred told me you were here. Do you mind if I join you?'

'Of course not, there's plenty of room' she answered, moving to a side bench.

As he made himself comfortable on the opposite bench she noticed a rather large blue grey mark on his leg.

The temperature was still too high, the atmosphere was too dry and rivulets of sweat trickled off her body. She jumped up and poured some water over the hot stones provided in a container near the door. Immediately a cloud of humid steam belched into to the air and filled the sauna.

'Are you trying to finish me off?' gasped the man. 'Open the door, quickly, I can't breathe.'

She fumbled for the handle and pushed the door half open.

'That's better,' the man groaned. 'First they tried to finish me off in the hospital and now I'm being boiled alive in a sauna. How would I explain that to my wife?'

She laughed. 'It's not that dangerous, I was only trying to lower the temperature. What happened to you in the hospital?'

He pointed to the mark on his leg. 'It's difficult to believe, but it happened during a walk in the woods. Bitten by a tick and I had noticed nothing. The insect had buried itself in my flesh and it wasn't until I was relaxing in the evening that I began to get a strange tingling feeling in my arms and then my shoulders. After ten minutes I was aching all over. My wife drove me to the Emergency Help department at the local hospital. The doctor asked me questions and made lots of notes. One of the questions that the doctor asked me was what I had been doing that day. He gave me some pills for the pain and sent me home. During the night I developed a high fever and felt incredibly weak. My wife was in panic and called an ambulance. In the hospital they put me on a saline drip and made various tests, but were mystified. Eventually one of the doctors reviewed my dossier and read that I had been on a walk through the woods. He was immediately suspicious, checked my legs, and found the small red swelling where I had been bitten. His suspicion confirmed, he quickly gave me a local anaesthetic and cut out the tick. He was just in time as it could have been fatal.

'How terrible,' said Sylvia sympathetically, 'I hope that you feel better know.'

'Yes thanks. I had to stay in hospital for three days followed by three weeks rest at home. He began to smile. 'Sitting next to such a charming young lady helps the recovery process. But! I didn't come to a massage parlour just for a sauna. May I make use of your services for a massage?'

'Of course, just stay here for ten minutes while I organise a room upstairs.'

She put on her working outfit and confirmed the reservation with Fred before preparing the massage room. As the man was not completely fit she made sure the room was warm enough, put an ash tray and a cold beer on the bedside table. She returned to the sauna, gave the man a bathrobe and led him up to the room. When they arrived he was breathing heavily from the exertion of climbing two flights of stairs.

'That took a lot more energy than I expected,' he said, as she helped him on to the massage table. 'I'm not as fit as I thought I was. Why don't we just relax and chat for a while.'

Sylvia sat next to him on the massage table while he told her his life story, smoked a few cigarettes and drank his beer. Occasionally he could not resist fondling her breasts and telling her how beautiful she was.

Eventually Sylvia noticed that an hour had passed. 'Sorry,' she said. 'But time flies and our time is up. You can continue further if you like, but I must first ask Fred for an extension.'

'No, that's not necessary. I think I have bored you enough and anyway it's time I went home.' As he left the room, he asked, 'I really enjoiney your company, how about a little drink at the bar before I leave?'

She tidied up the room, turned down the heating and put out the light. As she closed the door she could hear the buzz of conversation below, including the excited voice of Anita. It was a like a party atmosphere. Lively music was playing and the girls were all enjoying themselves, drinking wine and helping themselves to a variety of food spread out over the table.

As she walked down the stairs she noticed a tall, well built, man with black hair sitting at the bar, busy playing a dice game with Fred. Roy, the take-away man, was still there and seemed to be acting as the referee and prompting the players. There was no sign of her client. He was still busy in the changing below.

'Sylvia come and join us,' said Anita with a big smile. As it's a special day, we ordered some more food. But first let me introduce you to our friend Jamiel.'

The man at the bar stood up to shake her hand. 'I'm Jamiel,' he said, giving a slight whistle of approval. 'And you must be Sylvia. I'm certainly pleased to meet such an attractive young lady.'

He had dark eyes, a well manicured black moustache and a slightly tinted skin colour. He was rather flashily dressed, with a light camel coloured suit and a black shirt. There was a glint of a gold round his neck and a large gold watch on his wrist. He was probably of Middle Eastern origin but also quite good looking. He had a suave manner and obviously liked to display his attributes.

'Why don't you sit down and have a drink with me?' He patted the stool next to him. 'Anita! Would you mind giving this delightful young lady a drink?'

His voice was both persuasive and reassuring, combined with a compulsive look in his eyes. Sylvia found him exciting and somewhat irresistible. She joined him in a toast to Fred and Anita and their new enterprise. *Not the first toast or the last*, she thought.

Her curiosity was aroused. She carefully chose a moment when Fed and Anita were being distracted. 'So!' she said with an innocent look on her face. 'You are an old friend of the family?'

'Of course, I've known them for a few years.' He gave her a wink and lowered his voice. 'Well, actually, I knew Anita first. You know how it is.' He gave her a friendly dig with his elbow. 'She is an attractive woman, and at the time when Fred was busy at the casino she worked in my office for a while.'

She was about to ask more questions when she felt a tap on her shoulder. It was her client standing behind her, looking rather surprised at all the festivities. She took his arm, and they moved to a quieter spot, a few stools further along the bar, where he joined her for a coffee before leaving.

Jamiel was in no hurry to leave. He liked his beer and also liked being the centre of attention. When his glass was empty he would ask Anita for another round of drinks including something for the girls.

Sylvia was beginning to feel the effects of too much alcohol and decided to switch to soft drinks. It was early in the evening and clients could still turn up. She must keep a clear head.

She noticed that Anita was more lively than usual. She was wearing a provocative, low cut dress and held her shoulders back to accentuate the contours of her well endowed bosom. She hovered around the men at the bar, chatting in a flirtatious manner with Jamiel.

Fred had also drunk his share of beer, but showed no visible signs of its effect. He seemed to be amused by his wife's behaviour, but frowned occasionally when she was over exuberant. He had a notebook beside him on the bar and kept a careful tally of the drinks being consumed.

'Give me another one, darling.' Jamiel lifted his glass, his eyes fixed on Anita's cleavage. 'Being served by such a charming lady is one of the pleasures of life.'

'The night is young gentlemen,' Fred was obviously trying to calm the situation down. 'Why don't we play some poker? Anita, would you mind fetching some cards from the office?'

'Just a friendly game,' said Fred, as he dealt the cards. 'Why don't we limit the stakes to a maximum of five euros?'

The men soon focussed all their attention on the game and the girls relaxed in their usual places around the coffee table.

Against Fred the other players had little chance. He was a born gambler with plenty of experience. Even with the low stakes he had accumulated a significant amount of euros. Roy was the first to crack. 'Sorry guys,' he said. 'But I have to leave. I must go and check my personnel at the restaurant. I don't trust them on their own too long.'

Jamiel also looked relieved that the game had stopped. His wallet was suddenly empty and for the last few games he had to borrow some money from Fred.

As he left, Jamiel gave Anita a close hug. As he shook Fred's hand, he explained apologetically, 'Sorry old pal, I'm a bit short at the moment, but I will sort it out in a few days.'

Later while they were tidying up the bar Fred could be heard complaining to Anita, 'It's always the same with these so-called rich guys. Great at throwing their money around to impress the ladies, but rather reluctant when it comes to settling their bills. In any case I have made a note of what he owes me.'

When Sylvia arrived the next day, Fred's son Alfred was busy behind the bar cleaning the large mirror. Further along, by the coffee table, Puck and Laura were busy sorting out, and folding, towels and bath robes

'Good morning Sylvia,' said Alfred, cheerfully. 'I'm standing in for my father today. He has some business in Amsterdam and Anita took the opportunity to go with him to do some shopping.'

'I'm rather late,' she answered, I'd better go and change.'

'There's no hurry,' he said, putting down his cleaning material. 'Why don't you sit down while I make you a coffee? The other girls have had theirs already.'

She took off her coat and eased herself onto a stool. She could see a likeness to Fred in the young man's face. He also had black hair and a slight skin colour, but was much more sturdily built and, for his age, seemed to be quite self-assured. She noticed that he called Anita by her name and not mother.

'Doesn't this work interfere with your normal work?' she asked, stirring her coffee.

'Some days I'm free. I work part-time, at various jobs, but I am also studying accountancy. That is my long term aim.'

Their conversation was suddenly interrupted by a loud voice.

'Alfred! how about some music please? This place is like an old people's home'

She immediately recognised the voice of Hans van der Terp. She looked up and was amazed to see Hans and Chantal, both clad in bath robes, blatantly frolicking around at the top of the stairs. He had one hand on the stair rail and the other hand had disappeared under Chantal's robe. Chantal winked at Sylvia with a challenging smile on her face, like the cat that had got the cream. She waved as they disappeared in the direction of the massage rooms.

Alfred had a cheeky smile on his face as he rummaged through the collection of CDs. 'This should spoil their fun.'

She couldn't help laughing when he showed her the title – Famous Brass Band Marching Tunes.

It was obvious that Fred and his family were not very happy with Hans' involvement in the business. It was Fred's management experience that had allowed them to obtain a licence to start the business. They needed Hans to finance the premises but resented his interference in running the salon. They paid him rent and expected him to stay in the background. Unfortunately he was an old family friend and felt he was entitled to certain privileges, such as free drinks and occasional use of the girl's services. He would pay the girls directly but not pay the salon costs.

Half an hour later Hans and Chantal came down and sat next to each other on the settee behind the coffee table. They were still dressed in their bath robes and flirting with each other.

'Thanks for the romantic music,' Hans shouted to Alfred. 'Now I need a Bacardi and coke.'

'Sorry we don't have any Bacardi,' said Alfred, winking to Sylvia.

'What a shambles,' mumbled Hans. 'Give me a beer then, a malt beer.'

Alfred was about to take a beer to Hans when there was a loud bang on the front door. Without hesitation he sprang into action. He plonked the glass on the bar and ran to the door. He had heard from his father that some of the local people were not happy with the opening of a massage parlour in their neighbourhood. But this was going too far. He wrenched the door open, ready to deal with any aggressor and, instead, found himself face to face with an elderly man wearing a woollen cap, struggling to get out of an old motorised wheel chair and leaning on a crutch. The front wheel had apparently banged against the door.

'I heard about this place and decided to come along and see for myself,' the man said, standing up with the aid of his crutch. 'I live nearby and understand that you have some attractive young ladies working here. I'm looking for a small blond.'

'Well, then you better come inside.' Alfred could hardly hide his amusement. 'We cater for all ages.'

'Okay, okay.' He shuffled through the door and leant against one of the stools.

Sylvia smiled at him. She guessed that he was in his late seventies.

'Hey, young lady, what are you laughing at?' He snapped. 'Don't you have a nice blond friend?'

'Of course,' she said. 'I shall go and find her for you.'

She picked up the glass of beer and took it to Hans on her way to find Laura. Hans was now much more relaxed and he and Chantal were watching the events at the bar with amusement.

'Aren't you glad you're not a blond?' He grinned.

Sylvia found Laura down stairs tidying up one of the showers. 'There's a cantankerous old man upstairs asking for a little blond. Maybe you are interested. Puck is busy at the moment and you are the only other blond.'

Thanks,' she said. 'I'm not so little but I'm sure I can handle him.'

Laura new how to play the game and adopted a sensual walk as she approached the bar. She stopped and stood in a provocative pose in front of the old man.

He adjusted his glasses as he peered at her. 'I just want a normal massage,' he stuttered, suddenly looking nervous. 'I'm too old for any hanky panky.'

Laura put out her hand. 'Of course, but first let me help you downstairs where I can organise a shower for you.'

'I had a shower just before coming here,' he said indignantly. 'Just show me to the massage room.'

As Laura helped him up the stairs, slowly, one step at a time, he could be heard complaining, 'Why haven't you got a lift here? Are you really a blond? Have you also had a shower?'

It was once again quiet. Hans and Chantal disappeared downstairs to shower and dress, still behaving like immature teenagers. Puck and Laura were busy upstairs.

Sylvia sat by the bar chatting to Alfred. She found it interesting that such old men still liked to get some erotic arousal. 'You'd think that they would find other interests and save their money'

'It's difficult for us to put ourselves in their position,' said Alfred, looking cheeky again. 'We are young and healthy. Maybe when we get to their age we will want to convince ourselves that we are still fit and potent. They obviously continue to enjoy the pleasure of female company.'

'Yes and sometimes they want to prove they can still achieve everything,' she said, frowning. 'Then they need someone like Puck to keep them under control.'

Their discussion was interrupted by the next client. A good looking, young man had walked in. He was in his early twenties, had thick curly hair and bright eyes. Sylvia felt relieved. A young man at last. She instinctively straightened up and moved round slightly to display her legs.

Alfred had been well trained by his father. 'Welcome sir, can I help you? Most of our masseuses are busy at the moment, but this charming young lady is available. Her name is Sylvia. Why don't you discuss our arrangements with her?' He handed the menu book to Sylvia.

She moved closer. This was her chance to try out her persuasive talents. She sensed that the young man was rather insecure and nervous and that she must not be too pushy. She must put him at his ease. He seemed to be slightly embarrassed as they went through the alternative programs.

'Is this your first visit to a massage parlour? She whispered in his ear.

'Well, yes, actually it is. I've been thinking about it for a couple of weeks.'

'It's a new experience for me also,' she smiled. 'I've only been here a few days. Why don't we start with something that's not too complicated? How about three quarters of an hour body to body?'

'That sounds fine,' he said, breathing a sigh of relief.

After he had showered, she took him to her favourite massage room at the end of the corridor. As they passed the other rooms they could hear the voice of Puck giving instructions to her client.

'What do I call you?' She asked, as he handed her his bath robe and sat on the bed.

'Nathan, my name is Nathan.' He looked admiringly as she took off her robe, but averted his eyes as she removed her lingerie.

'Just lie down and relax, Nathan, leave everything to me.'

She felt a thrill of excitement. This was an important challenge for her, an innocent young man, completely at her mercy. She must take care not to destroy any fantasies he might have. Maybe this was the first time he had been alone with a naked lady. She must give him a wonderful experience.

She began with her usual massage treatment, hard, then tender, then titillating. Using plenty of oil and, at first, avoiding the erotic zone. Then she eased herself carefully above his body and moved her breasts lightly over his back.

He was breathing deeply. 'That's nice,' he murmured.

After a while she leaned back and, to put him at his ease, began talking to him about his education, his work and interesting topical events. She had quickly discovered that talking sympathetically to a client helped to break down any barriers between them and that, especially on long programs, it helped to pass the time.

Halfway through the program she moved to the side of the bed, saying; 'It's time to turn round.'

As he turned he looked admiringly at her figure. She moved back into position sitting on his legs. He had a very contented look on his face. He was quite handsome and had an athletic body. His penis was tantalisingly large. As she continued her massage treatment she felt a tingle of excitement. She took his hands and placed them on her breasts.

'You can also massage me sometimes if you like.'

He fondled her breasts as she leaned forward and moved her body sensually over his. It was extremely erotic. His arms were round her shoulders pulling her closer. His penis was stiff and desperate. She began to feel an irresistible sexual urge passing through her body. One small push and he would be inside her and they would be enveloped in a frenzy of passion.

But her self protective instinct was too strong. In the back of her mind she knew she must stay in control. She was too aware of the rules and the risks. A few minutes of passion could mean a lifetime of regret. She kissed him on his cheek and sat up.

'Our time is almost up,' she sighed. 'It's time to finish you off.' He closed his eyes as she played sensuously with his penis. She used all her tricks to build him up to massive ejaculation.

When he had left to take a shower, she returned to the bed. She could still feel his warmth. She closed her eyes and began to fantasise that he was on top of her and inside her. Her hand moved between her legs and she was soon overwhelmed by a powerful erotic orgasm.

She tidied up the room and returned to the bar. Hans was also there, drinking a beer, and this time chatting to Laura. He had apparently had enough of Chantal's continuous attentions and was relieved that she had been chosen by another Client.

Laura explained that after fifteen minutes her old man had fallen asleep and that she had let him rest until his time was up. He had been well satisfied and had even given her small tip before leaving.

It was early afternoon, Hans had left, Fred and Anita were still absent and Alfred and the girls were enjoying some pizzas ordered from the local Italian restaurant.

Puck was wearing her reading glasses, busy scanning through the national and local newspapers, checking the small ad's placed by competing massage salons.

'You must hear this,' she said to Alfred. Ticking, with a long manicured fingernail on a line in the Rotterdam Daily and reading out loud. *'Between five and seven-o-clock. Two masseuses for the price of one. Four hands erotic massage.'*

'Why don't we try something like that? We need to find a way to attract clients during the quiet period'

'You must ask Anita,' he answered, shrugging his shoulders. 'That's her speciality. She deals with all the advertising.'

Puck continued undeterred. 'This is a nice one.'

'Sensual body-to-body massage from a choice of gorgeous ladies.'

Sylvia laughed. 'Then we would be presented as lust objects.'

'That is what we are,' Laura couldn't resist joining in, 'and, to be honest, that's not a problem for me. If you are fortunate enough to have an attractive body why not make use of it. If someone has a talent for playing a violin he would be foolish not to take advantage of it.' She lifted her head, drew a deep breath on her cigarette and slowly blew out a plume of smoke, as if to emphasize the logic of her argument.

Sylvia was suddenly confused, she realised subconsciously that many people would agree with Laura. But, she wanted to be more than a lust object. She wanted to be able to impress her clients with her massaging skills and her conversational skills. It was more than just the satisfaction of sexual desire. She took an interest in current affairs and had travelled quite extensively. She knew how to empathise with people and make them relax. When she was finished with her clients they should leave feeling satisfied and happy.

'Why don't we call ourselves Entertainment Ladies? That could be a better title,' she suggested. 'It would cover a wide range of activities.'

'That might confuse our clients,' said Laura, with a cynical smile. 'Entertainment Lady! They might think we want to play darts or backgammon. And anyway, try telling that to your parents. They would still come to the wrong conclusion.'

Alfred realised that the some friction was developing in the conversation.

'A new girl is coming along later today.' He had obviously been waiting for the right moment to break the news. 'She could be a suitable replacement for Marieke.'

'She is not black, is she?' Chantal had joined them at the bar, with a large piece of pizza in her hand. She was worried that her unique position would be challenged.

'She is different. A southern type, that's all I know,' answered Alfred 'She could be an attraction to some clients.'

Sylvia's curiosity was aroused. She couldn't resist asking Alfred several times if he knew more about the girl.

'Be patient,' he said. 'You will soon find out. She is planning to bring a friend with her. They want to check us out first.'

It was quiet in the salon and all the girls were relaxing around the coffee table. Sylvia turned on the television to find an interesting program. Laura was eating an apple. Puck was still absorbed in the newspapers and Chantal seemed to be half asleep, probably dreaming about the next visit of Hans. Alfred was cleaning the floor behind the bar, which gave off a rather clinical aroma of bleach and lemon. In the background new-age music was softly playing. On the bar small candles were flickering inside coloured vases.

As she relaxed back into the soft cushions Sylvia closed her eyes and let her fantasies take over. She imagined she was trapped in a dimly lit cave, cut off from the real world outside, with a guard at the door. Clad in scanty underwear she was obliged to satisfy the needs of a variety of men, all young and handsome of course.

Her fantasies were rudely interrupted. Two young women walked through the front door, squinting into the dim interior. It must be the new candidates. They were both rather short and looked like they were in their late twenties. The one in front had a slender build and was wearing a long black dress and black shoes. She had black piercing eyes, long black hair and Arabian features. Her friend was more heavily built and dressed in a long dark brown coat and, surprisingly, wearing a head scarf. Everybody stared in amazement. A Muslim! What is a Muslim woman doing in a massage salon?

'I'm Moezerak and this is my friend Leila, said the thin one.' as Alfred approached them. She spoke with a pronounced foreign accent. 'We are here to see Fred.'

'Of course,' answered Alfred. 'We have been expecting you. Unfortunately my father is not here at the moment, but he should be back soon. I shall give him a call.'

They looked rather nervous as they sat on two bar stools near the door.

'He is on his way back from Amsterdam and has been delayed in a traffic queue,' explained Albert. 'He expects to be here in half an hour. Why don't you have some coffee while you are waiting?'

While he was organising the coffee, Alfred asked them where they came from.

'We are from Egypt,' said Moezerak, lighting a cigarette as she spoke. 'We live with friends in Holland. We are both learning the Dutch language, but it's difficult to find work here.'

'Why don't you look at our programs,' Alfred pushed a copy of the brown menu book along the bar.

They talked to each other softly, in a strange language, as they went slowly through the menu.

Fred eventually turned up and, with apologies for being late, took the two newcomers into his office. Ten minutes later, he asked Anita to give them a tour of the facilities. When they left they promised Fred to turn up the next day.

*T*he next day, when Sylvia arrived, they were both already there, sitting on the settee. The well built one had left her head scarf off and was wearing a brightly coloured, tight fitting dress that accentuated her bosom. The slender one had a long red party dress on. It had a short split on one side exposing the lower part of her legs.

Sylvia and Laura protested to Fred. 'Why do we have to wear these ridiculous white coats when they can wear what they like?

'They will only stay here on condition they can wear discrete clothing,' he said abruptly. 'You must understand they come from a different culture. We must make allowances.'

'Different culture? Bah!' snorted Laura. 'They live in Holland and are here for the same reasons as us. Rules are rules. If you want to change the rules, then it applies to us also. I have a sexy top and some short pants in my locker and that's what I will be wearing today. And anyway, these white coats are a joke. They are turning yellow and falling apart in the wash.'

Sylvia looked at her coat and nodded in agreement. It had lost its shape and some buttons were missing. She decided that she would also find a sexy outfit to wear.

Laura had achieved a break through. It was the end of the white coats. Fred did not complain and even had an admiring look on his face when she appeared in her tight fitting T-shirt and mini pants. Sylvia, Puck and Chantal looked at her enviously. From now on it would be different; every day would be a fashion show, a glamour competition between the ladies.

It was a strange day in the salon. The atmosphere had changed. It was too crowded for all the girls to sit on the settees at the same time. Sylvia and Laura spent most of the time sitting at the bar chatting to Anita. Chantal and Puck occupied the settee facing the bar. They knew from experience that it was the best location to be seen by men sitting at the bar. As newcomers the Egyptians were left sitting on the settee slightly hidden behind the coffee table.

A steady trickle of clients turned up and all the girls, except the Egyptians, were kept busy. Laura was especially popular, with her sexy outfit.

Fred did his best to promote the charms of Moezerak and Leila. Some men were obviously interested, but when they looked at them the girls modestly averted their eyes. They gave the impression that they would run a mile if a man touched them.

Eventually a client showed interest in Leila and Fred called her to the bar to introduce her face to face. She was the least shy of the two and even shook the man's hand. She agreed to a half hour basic massage and was smiling cheerfully as they disappeared downstairs.

Later in the afternoon Leila was chosen again. Although Moezerak was more attractive, it was not until early in the evening that she eventually succeeded. It was a busy period and only Puck and the two Egyptians were available. It was a man in his mid thirties who worked on an offshore oil platform and was seeking some relaxation. Fred explained that it was her first day and that he would be her first client. When Fred asked her to join them at the bar she actually seemed to be quite relieved. The man asked for some drinks so that they could quietly introduce each other and discuss a suitable program. After a few minutes the man beckoned to Fred pointing to a program in the menu. It was quite an extensive program, one and a half hours, including a session in the bubble bath. Fred, looking rather concerned, took Moezerak to one side, and briefly explained what was expected from her. She nodded in agreement, went back to the man and whispered something in his ear then took his arm and led him downstairs. Apparently she was not as prudish as everyone thought. Later, her client even asked for a half hour extension.

Fred had a satisfied look on his face as he leaned on the bar with a glass of beer. Enough customers were turning up and all the girls had been chosen. He knew that the more time they were kept occupied the less chance there would be for petty arguments or squabbles.

During a quiet period, between programs, Sylvia sat observing her boss. He was busy at the bar talking to Leila, who, according to Puck, he had only taken on as a manoeuvre to encourage Moezerak to stay. He was a devious old fox. He obviously viewed the new girls as exotic types. He could now offer the clients a wide range of choice.

She wondered in what categories he put the rest of them. He probably saw Laura, with her good looks, blond hair and sophisticated manner, as the star performer. Puck was obviously the motherly type, attractive to middle aged men, and Chantal was the exciting black queen.

And herself? How did he view her? With her attractive figure, long wavy red hair and long sexy legs. She was popular with the clients and was rapidly catching up in popularity with Laura; she was learning fast and had also become a star performer.

At last it was time to go home. It was Friday; she had survived the first week and she felt quite satisfied with herself as she collected her earnings. Now it was time to enjoy the weekend.

The weekend was over and she was looking forward to another week at the salon. She felt excited about the new challenge; *'no more white coats!* She had spent most of Saturday afternoon shopping in Rotterdam, looking for suitable clothes. She felt excited about the chance to dress up in seductive outfits and prance around tantalisingly in front of admiring men. She could do in reality what most other women could only do in their fantasies.

The choice was endless; low cut tops, short pants, tight fitting T-shirts, push-up bras, dangling earrings, glittering bracelets and necklaces. She had to restrain her impulses; she wanted to be sexy but not vulgar.

It was Monday and the bag she carried was bulging more than usual. When she arrived, the atmosphere in the salon was different. It was more lively than usual. Fred was behind the bar wearing a colourful batik shirt. The Egyptians were already there, wearing discrete but colourful dresses, long sparkling necklaces and several gold bangles on their wrists. They were apparently prepared for the competition. Laura was sitting at the bar, painting her nails. She looked stunning. Her sun tan was accentuated by her white top and short white pants.

Sylvia waved hello to everybody and rushed downstairs to change. She had brought two outfits, a white one and a red one. As Laura was already in white the choice was obvious. She put on a shiny, maroon coloured top with a built-in push-up bra, a matching short pleated skirt, black stockings and red high heels.

When she returned upstairs she got looks of amazement from the Egyptians and a whistle of approval from Laura.

Later when Puck and Chantal had turned up and changed their clothes, the salon had been transposed into a trendy glamour boutique.

'Well done ladies. You all look ready for battle?' Fred smiled cheerfully. 'Let's hope the clients appreciate your efforts.'

During the rest of the day all the girls got their share of clients.

For some clients it was a difficult choice. *Which of these lovely ladies shall I choose?* Sometimes there was even a bottleneck. There were six ladies available but only four massage rooms. The chosen girl then had the problem of persuading her client to wait until a room was free. This was a good opportunity for Fred to add the cost of a few drinks to the bill.

In her sexy outfit Sylvia was popular, especially with the younger men. But she tried to be choosy. She had quickly learned how to entice a client she fancied or to discourage anyone she considered undesirable. If a client turned up that she did not fancy she would look uninterested or hide behind a magazine.

Several weeks had passed and all the girls, including Moezarak and Leila, were still working enthusiastically at the salon.

A daily routine had evolved. Fred spent most of his time behind the bar, receiving and chatting to visitors, giving them drinks, controlling the background music, answering the phone, and trying to ensure that all the ladies were kept busy. He also kept the record of reservations and client payments, and monitored the time taken by the girls for each program. Anita controlled the supplies, the cleaning and the linen, and also did most of the administration work.

The girls themselves were responsible for cleaning up when necessary after they, or their clients, had used any of the facilities. They also organised their own food.

Every day in the salon was different, there were periods of heavy activity and periods of boredom, but there was always someone to talk to. The other girls were all friendly and talkative and there was always an air of suspense. Who was going to turn up next? What was going to happen next?

However, whenever a client was busy deciding who to choose, the friendship was temporarily suspended. Then it was war, every girl for herself, each having her own way of sending seductive signals to the client.

Sylvia enjoyed the work. It was different from a steady job, getting paid a fixed income irrespective of your performance. What you earned here was your own responsibility, it depended on your personality, your looks and you're massaging techniques. You were like a free agent. There was no contractual commitment. The working hours were flexible. The number of days and timing could all be negotiated and you could stop at any time at short notice. Of course, there was no long term security or social benefits. That was your own responsibility. But, for the short term it was satisfying.

Sometimes she still got butterflies in her tummy when she stepped through the door from bright daylight into the dim interior. The door was the portal between her two worlds. Each time she stepped through it she had to make a mental adjustment. Inside her name was Sylvia, the sexy temptress. Outside she was the office assistant working in an insurance office. Fortunately, at home she could easily keep up the pretence. Her work sounded so boring that her relatives and acquaintances soon gave up asking probing questions.

The flow of clients was also beginning to develop into a routine pattern. There seemed to be three distinct periods.

The first period was between opening time and late afternoon. The clients could be anybody who was not trapped into a regular eight to five job, clocking in and out at a fixed place of work. They would include company representatives, entrepreneurs running their own companies or retired men.

The second period was between office closing time and seven o clock. This was the quiet period, the time when most businesses were closed and all the men in Holland were either trapped in traffic queues, on their way home or eating their evening meals. This was the time when the girls could relax or arrange something to eat and watch television.

The third period was from about seven up to closing time. This was the busiest period, when anybody with the time and money to spare could turn up.

Laura was the biggest competitor for Sylvia. She was continuously in demand, and it soon became apparent that, even after the relatively short period they had been open, some clients had returned rather quickly for a second appointment.

Chantal who was still the least in demand, and rather envious, could not resist making a suggestive comment, 'According to me she is busy upstairs with the real thing. I think she has had some dubious experiences in the past. I heard that she spent some time working in a classy bordello.'

'Yes, but only as a telephonist,' said Leila, suddenly joining in. 'That's what she told me.' Her innocent looking dark eyes in her round pallid face looked questioningly at Chantal.

Leila was the type of person who would defend anybody who was unjustifiably accused. She was more sensitive than the tough Moezarak and it was a quality that seemed to make her attractive to some clients.

Sylvia had no wish to gossip about Laura. She still admired her. She knew how tempting it could be to give in to the demands of an attractive client. She also was trying to build up a few steady clients herself, ones who were friendly and loyal and would return on a regular basis. She was beginning to realise that to develop such a bond with clients it was necessary to be more relaxed. They chose you in preference to other the girls. They saw you almost as a personal friend and were willing to spend their hard earned money to spend time with you. In return they sometimes expected a bit more intimacy, even a little romance. She guessed that Fred and Anita would turn a blind eye; their main objective was to make a profit. At the same time she did not want to go too far, or to loose her self esteem.

Sometimes during a bath program with a favourite client, intimate and mutual fondling would begin. She had quickly learned that men also get satisfaction from giving pleasure to a woman. She would begin to get a warm sensation between her legs and feel the need to satisfy her own desire. Although she always stayed in control, she knew how to move her body over the man's body to increase her pleasure. And she did not resist when his hand moved between her legs and fondled gently. If she was in the right mood she would give in to her feelings and let herself be overwhelmed by a sensual orgasm.

She had followed Puck's advice and bought a mobile phone for business purposes only. Together with Anita she had also organised some business cards giving the days and times she was available and her mobile number. Her regular clients could now call her directly or SMS her for appointments.

Fred and Anita began to get a growing number of personal visitors. In addition to the three children, they seemed to have several other family members and friends from Indonesia. They tended to keep close contact and Fred often disappeared into his office for long telephone conversations. He was like a clan leader, giving them advice or listening to their personal problems. They began to treat the salon like a normal bar and sometimes one or more of them would turn up for a social visit and stay drinking and chatting until closing time. One particular friend, a small, dark skinned man, would turn up occasionally to play dice games with Fred. He was still a gambler at heart and sometimes money surreptitiously changed hands.

Unfortunately all these visitors were disconcerting for the girls and for the clients. After all, it was supposed to be a place of work, not a social club. While the visitors were dressed in normal clothes, the girls were expected to display themselves in their erotic clothing. It made them feel like animals in a zoo, being stared at by the visitors. Eventually the girls complained and pointed out that it was not good for business. Fred quickly changed his attitude and began to discourage his family and friends. He also began to entertain them in his office instead of at the bar. He installed more comfortable furniture and placed a gold lettered sign on the door: 'Private Office'.

Gradually changes began to take place in the salon. After the first few successful weeks, Fred and Anita were determined to build up the reputation of Body Line. They advertised widely in the local and national newspapers, trying out various texts, and they made a point of asking new clients which advert had attracted them.

They quickly realised the power of the internet and paid one of their friends to develop a web site. Each girl was asked to provide a description of their massage programs and their personal attributes. Those who were willing also provided photographs, and it was amusing to see how the photos were selected to promote the girl's charms without giving away their identity. They would have their head turned, or be wearing a large hat or mask to hide their faces.

Fred had heard from a few clients that a competing salon in Rotterdam was struggling to survive and that its services were declining. If one of its clients turned up he would turn on his charm, ply them with drinks and do his utmost to convince them that body touch was a much better choice.

The girls also became motivated by Fred's enthusiasm and began to feel part of the team, doing their best to promote the merits of the salon. Anita organised a weekly discussion with the girls to give them advice and to exchange ideas. How to improve their massaging techniques? How they should receive clients at the bar? How to persuade clients to return? How to deal with difficult or abusive clients? These discussions were also a good opportunity for the girls to air their grievances and to make suggestions for improvements.

Puck was gaining confidence and, without being asked, began to take on more and more activities, like an unpaid manager's assistant. As the oldest of the girls and the most experienced, she felt she was the most qualified for the work. She looked the part, had the right stature and radiated authority. At times when Anita was not around and Fred was busy in his office, she would take command of the bar and receive any clients that turned up. She gave them a coffee or a beer, explained the menu and introduced the girls. She was quite efficient and did not push herself at the expense of the other girls.

Fred still enjoyed chatting to the clients when they arrived, but as the boss, he considered it was not his job to serve nuts and coffee and was quite happy with Puck's help. She also began to answer the telephone and even took over some of Anita's activities, making sure that the washing was done on time and that the rooms were kept clean. The other girls had mixed feelings about her, but whilst they objected to her bossiness; they were relieved that they did not have to do the work themselves. Her most irritating habit was her tendency to talk too much, in a rather loud, penetrating and commanding voice. She talked to her clients at the bar until they got bored and left. She talked to Anita until she got bored and disappeared into the office. She talked to the girls until they got bored and turned on the television. They were all relieved when she was either busy with a client or had a day off.

If Fred happened to be busy in his office when a new client walked in, Puck would call out in a loud voice 'Fred! A client!'

Sylvia noticed with amusement that the tone of Puck's voice would vary, depending on her opinion of the man. If he was an impressive, well dressed gentleman her voice would be full of urgency. If she considered him to be rather ordinary or unrefined her voice would be a tone lower and less urgent. It seemed that Fred must have subconsciously detected the variation in urgency, as the time taken for him to come out of his office varied accordingly. But, if she thought he was reacting too slowly, Puck would complain out loud; '*He must be on the phone again*' and rush to the office and bang on the door with her fist. Client's, sitting at the bar, usually found her performance amusing, and the other girls would give her an encouraging cheer. In any event the ice would be broken and when Fred eventually emerged he had a sheepish grin on his face.

It was always the same ritual. The man received a drink on the house. Fred would ask him how he had found the salon and whether he been able to park his car easily. He would describe the programs available, pushing the most expensive ones. He would then lower his voice as he described the talents and charms of the girls; who was best at erotic tantra massage or at hard sport massage and who was the best company in the sauna or bath. His voice would drop even lower if the client was seeking even more entertainment. In such cases it was Puck or Laura who were eventually selected. Chantal the dark girl from Zambia was recommended as a tropical surprise from the Congo, Moezarak and Leila as the mysterious ladies from the east and Sylvia as the vivacious red head.

Sylvia had just arrived and was sitting at the bar drinking a coffee and reading the morning newspaper when the first customer of the day walked in. At first site he looked like any other mister average. He was of average height, in his mid forties, with dark brown hair, wearing glasses and dressed in a light grey suit. Puck immediately sprang into action, pushing the menu under his nose and going through her usual promotion routine. While he pretended to look through the programmes and listen to her chatter, he glanced a few times at Sylvia. Then he put down the menu, leaned close and whispered something in Puck's ear. For a second she looked surprised. Then a broad smile crossed her face as she shrugged her shoulders and nodded. After a few more words she moved round the bar, took his arm and led him downstairs. Sylvia looked at them in astonishment and was even more surprised when, as they passed, the man smiled and winked at her.

She finished her coffee and was absorbed in her newspaper when Puck returned and sat on the stool nest to her.

'Guess what, Sylvia,' she said softly. 'He is a client with special wishes; he wants you to join us in a double massage for one hour. Are you interested? We will both be paid the full amount.'

Sylvia hesitated for a moment. 'Well, I've never tried a double massage before, but it sounds like fun, so why not.'

'Good, I'll give you a sign when we are on the way up to the massage rooms.'

While she was waiting she began to feel excited about what was shortly going to happen. It was her first chance to take part in a four hands massage and she was intrigued with the idea of working with the experienced Puck.

As Puck led the three of them to the massage rooms the man had a smug look on his face, like a Pasha visiting his harem. He demanded to see all four rooms. The first one he found to be too close to the people downstairs, the second was too small and the third was not lavish enough. Their last hope was Sylvia's favourite room at the end of the corridor.

He looked round critically, and then nodded his head.

'This will do,' he said, as he handed his robe to Puck and eased himself on to the bed and put his hands behind his neck. It was obvious that he was not a stranger to massage parlours and he peered unashamedly at them

71

through his dark rimmed glasses, enjoying the show, as they tried to undress discretely. He had a sturdy build and he was already stiff and ready for action when they moved into position on each side of the table.

Puck was not intimidated. She immediately took control. She stood over him with her large bosoms drooping in front of his eyes and gave his weapon a quick slap with her fingers.

'Turn over and keep that thing under control,' she said in a loud sharp voice. 'We have only just started. You asked for a double massage and that's what you will get. You need some tough treatment to calm you down.'

Sylvia watched in amazement as, without any protest, the man did as he was told. She began to realise that his macho manner was only pretence and that he was the type that liked to be dominated by women. Puck poured some oil on his back and began to vigorously massage his neck, arms and shoulders as if she was massaging a rugby player.

She gave the bottle of oil to Sylvia and pointed to his lower half. She followed Puck's example and used all the strength in her hands to squeeze and manipulate his leg and thigh muscles. Then, almost without realising it, she had an urge to be sadistic, and ran her sharp nails under the soles of his feet. From his groans and bodily reactions it was clear that he was enjoying the treatment.

Puck varied her massaging from hard to soft and sometimes teased him by brushing her breasts over his body. At one stage, she even turned his head and instructed him to kiss her breasts. When they reached half time, she leant down to tell him that he could turn over. As he turned he muttered something to Puck who put her hand to her mouth in surprise.

'Is there a problem?' asked Sylvia.

'He wants to be blind folded and tied up,' she whispered. 'He apparently likes soft SM. Do you know if we have an eye mask somewhere?'

Sylvia was taken by surprise. 'Not as far as I know. You could ask Anita'

'I have a better idea,' she said. 'You get the cords from our bath robes while I go downstairs and find something in my locker.'

When she returned she waved some black material in front of the man's face and asked him if he had no objection.

Sylvia could hardly believe her eyes as she watched Puck lift the man's head like a sack of potatoes and cover his eyes with a pair of black panties. Next, they used the bath robe cords to tie his hands to the posts at the top end of the bed. He was now completely under their control. Puck seemed to be in her element and, for a few seconds, she stood over him like a surgeon about to operate. Then, with a sadistic look on her face, she began to tickle him vigorously around his waist.

His body gave an involuntary jerk. 'Aah! Stop that,' he groaned.

'Keep quiet.' she snapped. 'If you speak again without being asked you will have to be punished.' As a warning she squeezed one of his nipples between her fingers.

Sylvia found it a little creepy but also fascinating to see how Puck was able to dominate the man as she switched from erotic massaging one minute to rough, almost painful, manipulation the next. She concentrated on his penis, which seemed to be permanently stiff, using sensual caressing movements with her fingers until he almost reached a climax, then squeezing his balls and dragging her sharp nails over the shaft until he calmed down.

Puck gave her an encouraging thumbs-up sign. Then, with a wicked grin on her face, she put a finger to her lips as a signal to be quiet. She spread some oil over the man's tummy and with her finger wrote the words *'SUCKER'* in the oil.

Sylvia almost choked as she tried not to laugh out loud. Puck leaned back against the wall with tears of laughter running down her cheeks. 'Histoire d'O,' she spluttered. 'We are actresses in the film Histoire d'O. She bent over the man to see if he was still awake. He had a contented look on his face and was completely oblivious to their mischievous antics. 'It's time to finish you off,' she said. Squeezing one of his nipples hard with one hand and moving the other hand fast up and down on his stiff rod.

'I want to feel both of you. I want to feel all four of your hands,' he said excitedly.

Sylvia followed Puck's example and began to pinch his flesh and to squeeze his other nipple. He began to groan in a mixture of pain and pleasure until he suddenly lost control. Puck knew instinctively what was going to happen and pointed his penis in the direction of his chin trying to direct the spurts of white liquid as high up his chest as possible.

'That's the highest this week,' she murmured, as though it was a regular little game of hers.

When he had calmed down, Puck removed his blindfold and untied him, while Sylvia cleaned up his body with some tissues.

'Well done ladies,' he said, looking satisfied. 'You are very understanding. May I buy you both a drink before I leave?'

While Puck accompanied him down to the showers Sylvia tidied up the room. As she worked she reflected on the events that had just occurred and had conflicting emotions. She had been fascinated by the new experience but, at the same time, had found it strange to inflict pain on a person as a means of giving pleasure. She realised that she had taken her first step into the world of abnormal sex. But, she convinced herself, that if the client was happy, what did it matter? He got what he paid for.

As they sat with their client at the bar enjoying a well earned coffee, they found him to be quite a friendly and sympathetic person He was back to the normal mister average. Apparently it was only his sexual needs that were a somewhat unusual.

Later, when the he had left they were able to share their amusing escapades with the other girls and with Fred and Anita.

Fred seemed to be particularly interested. 'You handled the situation very well,' he said, stroking his chin thoughtfully. Then, looking at Anita, he continued; 'Maybe we should be better prepared for this sort of client in the future. Don't you think we should organise some special equipment.'

'Good idea,' answered Anita. 'We could organise a special SM bag and keep it upstairs near the massage rooms. Any suggestions for what we should put in it?'

Puck's eyes lit up with enthusiasm. 'We need an eye mask, some ribbons or cord, some manacles, and some clothes pegs.'

'What do we need clothes pegs for?' Asked Sylvia innocently.

'To pinch their skin or nipples with, of course.' It was the loud voice of Chantal who had been listening in the background. 'They must be the sort of pegs that are held in place with springs, the bigger the better. And! Don't forget a whip and some candles for the hot wax treatment.'

Her enthusiasm suggested that she would be only too happy to try out the SM bag on a few of her customers.

A few weeks later, the Egyptian girls, Moezarak and Leila, suddenly stopped turning up. When asked why, Fred shrugged his shoulders, as if he couldn't care less.

'C'est la vie,' he remarked, when Sylvia said she missed them. 'I have no idea why they stopped. They were never very popular, so maybe they didn't earn enough to make it worthwhile.'

Later she heard from Puck, that Moezarak's boyfriend had recently been released from prison and he had discovered, by accident from Leila, what sort of work they were doing. The poor Moezarak had been beaten black and blue and was hiding in a safe house.

Sylvia and the other three girls, Puck, Laura and Chantal, were quite happy with the new situation. They now had less competition and each of them had a steady flow of customers.

However, it was too good to last. When all four girls were present it was no problem, they could easily accommodate all the clients that turned up. But, for various reasons, including the long opening times, each of them found it necessary to sometimes take time off. Occasionally when only two or three girls were present, and if they happened to be occupied when more clients turned up, some had to be turned away.

For Fred of course, this meant missed opportunities and he immediately began to advertise for new girls.

Within a few days a new candidate arrived, one that would prove to be a real challenge for the other girls. She was an attractive young lady with long blond hair and a sexy body. Although she was rather shy and inexperienced Fred engaged her immediately. He called Sylvia into his office to introduce her.

'This is Ariella,' he said. 'She is a complete beginner, just like you when you started, so I thought it would be a good idea to let you show her around, introduce her to the other ladies and explain the routines here.'

'Of course, with pleasure' said Sylvia, shaking the new girls hand enthusiastically. 'Just follow me. First I'll show you round, then we can meet the other girls.'

As she guided her round the salon Sylvia could not resist enquiring about the girl's background. Apparently she had a boyfriend who was in the navy and he had just been assigned on a tour of duty to the Mediterranean. She had been working as a shop assistant and was now looking for something more adventurous.

'I suppose your boyfriend must not know what you are up to?'

'No, of course not,' she answered, nervously. 'But there's no way he can find out, I hope!' As far as he's concerned I'm still working in a shop.'

'And anyway,' she continued naively, 'it's only massage work isn't it? So he shouldn't be too jealous.'

Puck and Chantal gave the new girl an encouraging welcome. Laura, however, was rather aloof. She was obviously worried about the new challenge: *Another blond! And much younger!*

It lasted several days before Laura accepted Ariella as one of the team. She was determined to keep her regular clients from being tempted to try the younger intruder. She began to wear even more daring and evocative clothing and rushed to welcome her clients directly they entered the door.

Sylvia found Laura's behaviour rather comical, but she also noticed the increased competition, she was no longer the youngest of the team. The younger clients, who preferred girls of their own age, now had a choice between a young blond and a young redhead.

Fortunately Fred and Anita had stepped up their advertising campaigns and were attracting more clients, and they were all kept reasonably occupied.

The main objective of the girls was to build up as many regulars as possible. There seem to be two main types of regulars. There was the rather shy, insecure guy who seemed to be lacking something in his life, either having problems with his partner or having no partner at all. He would be seeking consolation in a substitute friendship combined with an erotic experience. The other type was the successful guy, the one who considered himself to be a bit of a playboy and entitled to enjoy some reward for all his efforts in life. He would tend to be more sexually aggressive. Both types tended to become emotionally attached to one girl only.

All the girls became possessive about their regular clients and tended to give them nicknames. This became necessary because most of them preferred not to use their real names and would choose the first alternative that came into their head, such as; Bob, Bill or John. As a result there would be several clients with the same name.

Sylvia got into the habit of identifying her regulars by their profession or background, such as; 'The Professor,' from the local university, 'The Italian,' an entrepreneur from Italy, 'The IT man,' from the computer industry, 'The Project Manager, from the oil industry, 'The Developer,' from the local council and 'The Super,' from the police department. Even Fred and Anita began to use the same nicknames when talking about clients.

Although it was not openly acknowledged by any of the girls, it was only to be expected that some of the long term and loyal regulars would eventually receive more intimate treatment. Body to body massaging is, after all, an intensely erotic and arousing activity and to suddenly stop when a climax is imminent is unnatural and sexually frustrating, for both the client and, sometimes, for the girl.

So far Sylvia had managed to keep her regulars satisfied with massages in accordance with the official programs, although several had given clear signals that they would be very happy to take a step further. She realised that, eventually, she would be faced with the choice of either loosing a client or satisfying his needs.

With some of her favourite clients, the ones she found physically attractive, she already had difficulty in restraining herself. She even began to fantasise about letting loose and having a wild session. It was a boundary yet to be crossed. It was just a matter of time!

Laura was particularly successful in building up a large clientele of regulars, mostly middle aged men. Puck had more success with the older men. They both seemed to have a talent to make each client feel special and to convince him that he was their favourite.

Sylvia was rather choosy and selective in which clients she encouraged to become regulars. She felt superior to the other girls. She knew she was the most intelligent and had the most attractive body. She considered herself to be 'Officer Class' only. She was in demand and could afford to be selective. She knew how to discourage any guys she considered to be of 'the lower ranks.' She was the one that made the choice not them.

There developed a sort of an unspoken agreement between the girls not to intentionally pinch each others regulars. Sometimes, however, if his regular girl was not present a client would be tempted to choose another girl and this was generally accepted.

Most of Sylvia's clients were very loyal and if she happened to be occupied or absent when they turned up they would either wait, or leave and return another day. To avoid disappointment she persuaded most of them to call and make an appointment in advance.

She understood that it was in most men's nature to desire some variation, after all that's why most men came to the salon in the first place, and if one of her regulars began to show interest in another girl she would pretend that she had no objection.

"Why don't you try her out, then you might appreciate me more,' she would say. 'But, preferably not when I am around.'

If they asked her permission first, she didn't mind too much. But, if they were sneaky and she found out later, she would be furious, as if she had been betrayed.

A smartly dressed man in his early fifties began turning up regularly and taking long programs with Puck. Whenever he walked in, Puck would be waiting for him, she would rush to welcome him and lead him directly downstairs

During one of his visits Laura and Sylvia happened to be sitting at the bar chatting to Fred.

Laura nudged Sylvia with her elbow. 'Have you noticed anything different about Puck lately?'

Sylvia frowned thoughtfully for a few moments 'Well, now you mention it, she does seem to be rather subdued and I haven't heard her big mouth quite so much.'

'Didn't you notice how she behaved just now when her client turned up? She is normally quite bossy and calls them by their first names, but with this guy she is more restrained. She even calls him Mr. Jackson.'

Even Fred, who never missed a trick, couldn't resist joining in. 'That's right, Mr. Jackson is turning up twice a week, and, he always calls in advance to make sure Puck is available.'

'He's certainly having some sort of effect on her,' said Laura. 'She hardly ever makes our coffee any more and sits around looking confused half the time.'

'It looks like some sort of relationship is developing,' said Fred, looking concerned. 'I'll ask Anita to keep an eye on her,'

After her client's following visit, Puck remained at the bar, looking rather flushed.

'Is everything alright?' asked Anita

'Well, actually I'm not sure. I'm getting a bit overwhelmed.' she answered, looking relieved that she had found someone to talk to. 'My client, Mr Jackson, is getting too keen on me. He's quite rich and keeps buying me presents. He thinks he can buy me.'

She extended her arm to reveal a gleaming gold bracelet.

'So why don't you make the most of it?' Anita looked at the bangle in astonishment. 'It's not every day that one of our girls gets so much attention.'

'I know, but as well as being generous he is also rather dominating.' She looked offended. 'He sometimes criticises the way I dress and even the way I talk. He says I chatter a too much.'

'Don't worry about that.' Anita tried to reassure her. 'Most men criticise their partners. It's a way of proving their masculinity. But, what's more important is, you do find him attractive?'

'Well, yes, very much. But that's not all,' she continued. 'Today he told me that he wants to take me to Bali for a long holiday and insists that I buy a skimpy bikini. He is getting the tickets next week. I'm not sure what to do. Everything is happening so fast. He wants a permanent relationship.'

'If I were you, I would think seriously about his offer, after all you are not so young any more. And, you still have a good figure, so wearing a bikini is not a problem. The beaches there are full of overweight tourists, sunbathing half naked.'

'But what do I do about my friend in Germany? The one I told you about. We have sort of understanding that I visit him once a year.'

'You mean the guy who rents a small apartment over the garage where he works? That seems to be rather a casual friendship. It doesn't sound like there is much future in it. You can always keep him as a friend.'

'You are probably right, she said brightening up a little. 'But what about Body Touch? How will you manage without me?'

'Don't worry about that, your future could be at stake. Just relax for a few minutes while I go and explain the situation to Fred.'

When Anita returned, she put her arm on Puck's shoulder. 'It's no problem. Fred agrees that your happiness is the most important. We appreciate all the help you have given us. But this opportunity is too good to miss. You must go to Bali. If things go wrong you are always welcome back here.'

At the end of the week Fred and Anita organised a surprise farewell party for Puck. It was her last day. Mr Jackson was invited and proved to be a really nice character. Puck had got over her misgivings and was beaming with happiness. It was almost like an engagement party. All the girls had contributed to a gift, and she was sent off on her dream holiday with a digital camera.

$\mathcal{T}$he salon door opened and all the girls' heads turned instinctively, in anticipation of the next client. Instead, a woman walked in and they all froze in amazement.

She had just stepped out of the front page of a classy woman's magazine. She appeared to be in her mid thirties, tall, slender and elegantly poised. Her make-up was immaculate and her clothes were modish and perfectly matched. Her shiny, wavy brown hair bounced over her shoulders. She was obviously a woman of the world, used to a life of luxury.

Her large dark eyes swept round the salon, and focussed on Anita, who was standing behind the bar.

'May I speak to the person in charge?' she asked, in a cultured and confident voice.

'Why don't you take a seat, while I find my husband?' answered a bemused Anita.

As she sat down, she opened her YSL handbag and a perfectly manicured hand extracted a cigarette and gold lighter.

Sylvia noticed the sparkle of a blue sapphire as she lit her cigarette, took a puff, and moved her hand elegantly away from her face. A slight smile indicated that she knew what they were all thinking.

'What's a lady like that doing in a place like this?' whispered Laura. 'She must be getting bored with life.'

'Maybe she is looking for some excitement,' answered Sylvia, watching her with admiration and remembering her own first day.

Fred emerged from his office looking enthusiastic.

'Can I help you madam?'

'Well, it's rather personal,' she said, lowering her voice. 'May we discuss this in private?'

'Of course, please follow me.' Fred showed her to his office while Anita organised the coffee.

Half an hour later they watched as he escorted her to the door. They were surprised when she turned, smiled and waved her hand in their direction

As he returned to the bar, Fred faced a row of questioning faces.

'You may not believe it ladies, but you have a new colleague. Her name is Alexandra and she is starting next Monday. She will be working here three or four days a week'

'Does she really need to work in a salon, like this?' Laura was unable to resist asking the question.

'The same question can be asked of all you ladies,' he snapped. 'Its perfect timing, we need someone to take Puck's place, and I expect you all to help her settle in.'

Monday arrived and so did Alexandra, no longer the front page model but still a sensual and attractive lady. She now wore a black tight fitting dress and black high heels together with dangling gold ear rings and some gold bangles on her arm. She was using an exotic French perfume. She would undoubtedly be an asset to the salon.

Anita took her time showing her the facilities and explaining the services she was expected to offer. The newcomer's confident manner during her first visit had apparently been an act of bravado. She now looked slightly apprehensive as Anita introduced her to each girl in turn.

Laura, turning on the charm, offering her a cigarette and starting a friendly conversation, determined to extract the life story behind the façade. Alexandra responded coolly, keeping the conversation superficial. She was not going to be trapped into exposing her personal details to a perfect stranger.

Sylvia was intrigued. She could visualise herself in ten years time. Here was the type she could emulate and aspire to, and she was sure they would eventually become friends. But she was also worried; another 'Officer Class' lady; one that could be an attraction to some of her best clients.

As the day progressed a steady flow of clients arrived, and all the girls were chosen, including Alexandra. She had adapted quickly to her new situation. She was not here for the money only. She was in her prime, the kind of woman most men could only dream of, and she was fully aware of her physical assets. Her normal life was obviously too mundane. Like Sylvia, she was here for adventure, to satisfy some latent sensual desire, to satisfy a basic urge to display and make more use of her curvaceous body, to be admired and to be given compliments by appreciative men. Life was short and to be enjoyed, before the years took their toll.

Fred, of course, was looking happy and self satisfied. His sweet shop was now full of appetising goodies and, like little boys with too much pocket money; some customers would be tempted to try them all.

There was a heightened sense of competition in the salon, and later that evening when one of Sylvia's regulars, The Professor from the university, turned up, she found herself rushing to the bar to greet him, to get there first! Then, feeling slightly embarrassed, she realised that she was acting just like Laura did, when the young blond arrived. Even so, as she led him past the other girls on the way to the changing room, she noticed his eyes dwelling for a few seconds on Alexandra. A dangerous few seconds.

The Professor was good looking, in his mid forties and sexually high key. He turned up quite often, at least once a fortnight, and always took a one hour program. He was one of her favourites and she always felt a surge of excitement when he arrived.

They did not waste time in the sauna or whirlpool but went directly to the massage room. This meant a whole hour in close contact on the bed. At the beginning she did her best to keep him calm, by sitting firmly on his back and trying to prolong her massage treatment. But he was far too impatient and too aroused. She could not prevent him turning round and they were soon enveloped in more intimate and mutual body to body movements and erotic fondling.

Even in the middle of this passion she could not help getting a niggling feeling in her mind. *Was she doing enough to keep him satisfied? Were their sessions becoming too routine? Should she go a step further?*

But her doubts quickly passed. No she decided! If he was being tempted to try someone else, why should she worry, there were plenty more pebbles on the beach. She realised that doing everything would not diminish any desire he might have for variety, and would only cause her more regret.

A few days later Sylvia's fears proved justified. She was leaving one of the massage rooms after finishing with a client when she heard familiar voices below. Her heart beat faster as she peered over the banisters. He had turned up again, only this time he was sitting at the bar with Alexandra. His face was close to hers as they studied the menu together. Her sexy black dress, her exotic perfume and her witty comments were apparently irresistible. Fred was busy filling their glasses from a bottle of wine, something which The Professor had never offered her.

She went back into the massage room to recover. She was shocked. Her ego was dented. How could he prefer her, an older woman? It took her several minutes to calm down. Then, she took a deep breath, checked herself in the mirror, pushed her shoulders back and went down stairs. She would show them she didn't care. She had more than enough admirers.

On purpose she went directly to the bar and smiled at the Professor. He looked uncomfortable as he gave her a weak, embarrassed smile in return and quickly left for the sauna with his new trophy.

Fred poured them both a glass of wine from the vacated bottle. 'Cheers,' he said, raising his glass. 'Don't worry Sylvia you are still the top performer. These men pay a lot of money and sometimes can't resist trying out the other goodies. You ladies mustn't get too possessive. It's better for all of you if they can switch around here rather than go to another salon.'

'I suppose you are right,' she answered, still feeling a bit peeved. 'They are all basically polygamous animals.'

It was another successful day for the girls. Alexandra looked especially pleased, it was only her second day and she had been chosen by four men, all of whom promised to return.

'She's succeeding too well,' muttered Laura, still feeling threatened. 'She has more class than Puck, and is younger and better looking.'

'Don't worry too much,' Sylvia had also been busy and had almost forgotten The Professor incident. 'She's quite an asset for the salon and I'm sure we shall all benefit in the end.'

Alexandra was unaware of any resentment she might have caused as she joined the others round the coffee table. She was friendly and relaxed and her posh accent seemed to have disappeared.

'You are doing quite well for a beginner,' said Anita. 'Have you tried massaging before?'

'Not as a job,' she said enthusiastically. 'But when I first got married I used to massage my husband and, although that was a few years ago, I still remember a few tricks.'

'Does he know you working here?' asked Sylvia.

'No! Certainly not! But fortunately, for the time being, he is away working in South America. He is on a two year assignment and gets two flights home a year. I could have gone with him, but he is a workaholic and I would be left on my own most of the time in a strange land.'

'If I had a rich husband I wouldn't be sitting here,' grunted Laura.

Well, nobody is forcing you to sit here.' Alexandra reacted instantly. She was not going to be easily intimidated. 'If you don't like it there must be plenty of other jobs you can do.'

Everybody laughed. Laura frowned, quickly lit a cigarette and kept quiet.

'What attracted you to this work?' asked Sylvia, getting curious.

'When I left school I worked for several years as a secretary. I stopped work when I got married, and began to accompany my husband on his overseas assignments. Now I'm stuck at home, doing nothing. I find it so boring. I don't want to work full time and I want to do something exciting. When I saw your advert, I thought; what the hell! it could be fun, why not give it a try.'

Alexandra stayed, and although her superior manner discouraged some men, she quickly accumulated a number of steady admirers. They were mostly respectable business men, between the late thirties and the mid fifties. Sometimes, however, a younger man would be tempted by the excitement of a massage from a mature and experienced lady. Sylvia's fears that she would lose many of her regulars did not materialise. She was, after all, much younger and just as attractive. They soon became friends and enjoyed exchanging stories about their travels.

The salon was becoming popular. Sometimes clients had to wait their turn, at the bar, or sit in their bath robes on the settee. Sylvia frequently served behind the bar and had quickly learnt how to keep the customers relaxed with her amusing chatter and her cheeky repartee.

In the middle of the afternoon she was busy rinsing out some glasses when an attractive, neatly dressed young man with curly hair walked in and sat at the bar. He was staring at her.

'Can I help you? She asked, giving him a big smile.

'I think you must be Sylvia,' he replied, looking into her eyes.

'Yes, I'm Sylvia, how do you know my name?' She found his eyes penetrating and disconcerting.

'My older brother told me about you. He was here a few weeks ago. He said he had a wonderful time. He gave me a good description of you and made me intrigued. I've never tried a massage before, but I was so impressed I decided to find out for myself.'

He extended his hand. 'My name is Jonathan. Do you have some time for me?' he asked politely.

His voice was deep and self assured. He was very good looking and had a sturdy build. As she took his hand she felt a sudden, irrepressible spark of desire. A mental picture of their two naked bodies in close embrace flashed through her mind. As she handed him the little brown book she realised her hand was trembling.

'Why don't you suggest a suitable program?' he said, putting the menu back on the counter. You are the expert.'

'Well, if you have enough time, we could take an hour body to body.' She tried to sound casual, as though it was a normal everyday activity, but her hormones were now working overtime and she couldn't resist persuading him into to take a long and sensual program.

'Perfect. I'm in your hands.' He looked relieved.' Lead the way.'

When he removed his bath robe she looked admiringly at his athletic body and could sense the aroma of a subtle masculine perfume. She did not resist when he put his hands on her shoulders, gently turned her round, unhooked and removed her bra, then eased her panty downwards. She felt a tingle of excitement as he pressed against her, kissed her on the neck and gently caressed her body. There was an instantaneous spark between them, a sort of mutual attraction, as though they were already intimate friends.

He gave her a little squeeze round the waist, took her hand and pulled her onto the bed, then turned on his face and closed his eyes. Without saying a word she moved over his body, sprinkled some warm oil on his back and began her massaging routine.

He was completely relaxed and breathing slowly as her hands moved around his body varying from gentle rotating movements over his back and around his neck, to hard pressure and manipulation of his arm and leg muscles. She took her time, applying all the techniques she had perfected over the last few weeks. She had developed the ability to sense the mood of her victim through her finger tips, as though a magical flow of energy was passing between them. She could induce a passive trance like state or maintain an active response. She could control the degree of intimacy and arousal.

She sensed the pent up energy in the man below her, waiting to explode. Temptation was growing inside her but she forced herself to stay away from the erogenous areas, to continue the pretence of a therapeutic massage.

Eventually, it was time to take the next step, to move to the sensual stage. The stage that, once set in motion, would be continued until the ultimate climax. She lowered her arms and with gentle pressure slid her oily body over his, up and down, round and round. Then she lifted herself slightly until only her nipples were making contact and moved them over his back and bottom. He responded immediately with a groan of enjoyment. She dribbled some oil on his buttocks and massaged them gently with her fingers. Instinctively his legs moved apart inviting her to teasingly fondle his balls.

The result was instantaneous; he was wide awake and, in one move, sat up on the bed, put his arms round her and gave her a passionate kiss on the mouth.

'That was amazing,' he said. 'I was almost in a trance. Now I think it's your turn for a massage. You deserve a rest.'

He pushed her gently but firmly down on the bed, underneath him. As his body moved over her she could see that he was well endowed and that it was stiff and erect. She felt an incredible urge to surrender. For weeks she had controlled herself, keeping to the rules, delaying the moment when she would succumb to her desires. It was a barely concealed secret that Laura and Chantal sometimes went all the way to satisfy their favourite clients.

The right moment had now arrived. It was time to yield, to be dominated, to be completely overwhelmed, to give in to whatever takes place. Time to forget the rules.

She shut her eyes as he began to move his hands tenderly over her body. He was obviously inexperienced, but his amateurish movements only increased her excitement. He began discretely, carefully avoiding the sensual areas, waiting for a signal of encouragement. She moved his hands onto her breasts and from then on nature took over.

He fondled her breasts and kissed her nipples. She relaxed and parted her legs as his hand moved between her thighs. This was mutual lust, a desire to penetrate and to be penetrated. She sensed an uncontrollable release of lubrication as she felt his fingers enter and move around inside her body. She moaned with pleasure as his head moved between her legs and she felt his tongue moving over her clitoris.

After what seemed an eternity, she pulled him upwards until they were in close embrace, then, rolled on top. She poured some oil in her hands and onto his penis and began her tantra routine. The routine she had perfected on so many of her clients. She moved her hands sensually up and down, round and round, pausing when he seemed to be losing control, then, continuing up to the next high point.

Even in the midst of all this passion, she remembered the risk of a first encounter and reached out to the bedside table, opened the drawer and took out one of the little packages. As she handed it to him he nodded in agreement and ripped it open. She put her fingers round his stiff penis and played sensually until it felt like an iron bar. She could not resist increasing his excitement by lowering her head and putting it into her mouth, as far as possible. He was now desperate for the final performance, and she held it erect as he clumsily tried to roll the condom into place.

'Let me do it,' she said, pushing his hands away. 'It helps if you use it the right way round.'

'Yes teacher. Go ahead and help yourself.' He lowered his arms and shut his eyes. 'We still have plenty of time.'

Fortunately she had prepared for this moment. She had practised a few times, on a large candle, and was amazed how expertly she was able to position and roll it securely into place. Now they could both enjoy themselves without any disconcerting worries in the back of their minds.

She felt an exhilaration of power as she moved into a dominating position above him. She paused for a few seconds, to make him desperate, then, lowered herself onto his weapon. She moved slowly at first, enjoying the sensual feeling of a having man's penis inside her. Then as she got hotter and hotter she moved faster and faster. Eventually, when he was getting too close to losing control, he stopped her moving, threw her on her back and moved above her. She instinctively opened her legs wide and guided his weapon with her hand as he pushed it gently inside. She responded by putting her arms around his waist and forcing him to push harder. He did his best to vary his tempo and paused a few times to prolong their enjoyment. But, their bodily urges were unstoppable. They were like wild animals lost in a frenzy of body movements, and were soon swept into a simultaneous climax.

They collapsed alongside each other and lay still for several minutes recovering, in each others arm. It was late afternoon and daylight flickered through the Venetian blinds.

Their peace was rudely interrupted when somebody outside tried to start their car several times without success.

Sylvia laughed. 'Outside everything is grey and ordinary. In here it is a world of fantasy and pleasure.'

'Most people don't know how to make the most of their lives,' he sighed.

'What do you so for a living?' she asked, sensing he was talking from experience.

'I'm a doctor, and I work in a group practice. I meet so many people with emotional problems. Often self created. It's nice to escape sometimes.'

'Well, you know where to escape to now,' she giggled.

'Yes, I certainly do, but unfortunately it's time for me to leave; I probably have a few patients waiting for me.'

As they stood up, he put a hand on her shoulder, looking a little concerned. 'I had such a wonderful time, but I hope I didn't push you into anything against your will.'

'Not at all, I'm glad it happened. It was so spontaneous. I had a fantastic time.'

He gave her a peck on the cheek. 'From now on you are my friend. Next time we should be more relaxed so that we can get to know each other better.'

Sylvia drifted through the rest of the day in a rosy haze. She had no regrets about what had happened. She had crossed a barrier and it gave her a kick. It was harmless enjoyment, the satisfaction of mutual lust. She had aroused a fire within herself that could no longer be extinguished.

Fred looked on in a mixture of amusement and concern as she hummed to herself behind the bar.

Over the next few days she enjoyed her work even more. During quiet periods she would daydream about her encounter with her darling Jonathan and look forward to his next visit. It gave her a warm and yearning feeling in her body. She was glad that the first time that it had happened in the salon was with such a charming young man. She began to get more enjoyment from the sexual attentions of her regulars, especially the younger ones. She was proud of her body and welcomed their attention when they kissed her breasts or fondled between her legs. But it always stopped before the critical point. She knew she must control herself but was beginning to feel sexually frustrated. She began to fantasise about further similar encounters.

A couple of weeks had passed and on the surface the business was thriving. For the girls it was paradise, a smart environment had been provided for their use, they could virtually decide when and how many hours they worked, and as long as enough clients turned up they had were happy. Their rewards were related to their own performance. If they were not satisfied they could easily leave and, if necessary, find some other work.

For the so-called partners it was a gamble yet to pay off. Cracks were appearing in the façade. What began as a friendly partnership, in what seemed to be a guaranteed profit making enterprise was fast changing into a more formal business relationship based on contractual agreements and commitments.

Tensions were building up. Hans van der Terp had invested most of his capital in the building and its furnishings and expected to receive a good return from the rental payments. He still felt entitled to visit when he wanted. Sometimes when the rent wasn't being paid on time he also felt justified to probe into the running of the business and to give advice to Fred. He began to make insinuating remarks about his management of the salon, sometimes based on information he had heard from the girls; *Fred sat too often in his office, used the phone too much, entertained his friends too much and drank too much.* There was always a girl with a chip on her shoulder happy to pass on her grievances.

They had been over optimistic about the profits and the costs had been underestimated. Fred was struggling to pay his monthly instalments. The bills were piling up; outstanding bills from the contractors and suppliers during the renovation, energy and insurance costs, maintenance, licensing fees, cleaning, advertising, accountant, lawyer, taxes. He realised that he must economise. At the slightest excuse the heating would be turned down. The girls would be charged for their drinks and asked to help in the cleaning, notices were put up reminding the girls to turn off the lights, the sauna and the whirlpool when not in use.

Anita considered the possibility of opening on weekends, but soon gave up when she discovered that the girls were not happy about giving up their free days; they worked long hours already, and it was also doubtful if they would attract enough clients to cover the additional costs.

Sylvia, Laura and Alexandra, who were by now were all good friends, on the same wavelength, would watch intrigued when Hans walked in. They would try to judge by his manner and the expression on his face which of the three options it was this time. Was it a friendly social visit? Was it business related? Or, was it to satisfy his carnal needs?

At times when their financial problems had temporarily subsided Hans would be welcomed as the steadfast family friend. The atmosphere in the salon would become relaxed, the drinks would flow and Roy would be called to deliver some take away. Fred would sit behind the bar with his beer and cigarettes and pretend to ignore the flirtations between Hans and Anita. Maybe he saw it as a way of placating Hans, softening him up in regard to their financial difficulties.

The girls were curious about the previous relationship between the two, but it remained a closely guarded secret. Whatever it had been, the effect on Anita whenever he turned up was dramatic. It boosted her ego. Here she was, surrounded by attractive ladies having endless romantic encounters and here was one of the most attractive men focussing his attentions on her on and paying her compliments. She would wear a low cut dress and disappear into the office to fix her hair and make-up. She would drink too many glasses of wine and giggle at his remarks like an infatuated teenager.

He would have the opposite effect when his visit was for other purposes. He would try to time his visits for pleasure, with Chantal or one of the other girls, when Anita was absent. If she happened to be present there would be an embarrassing greeting as he quickly went past her to collect his selected masseuse and disappear down to the changing room.

Anita would pretend she didn't care, but her face looked sad and resentful as she looked up in the direction of the massage rooms. Sylvia would do her best to console her. She would join her at the bar and they would share a bottle of wine. She would try to keep her distracted by looking through her family photograph album, which she kept in the office. Anita made good use of her digital camera and frequently updated the album. She even reserved one section for snaps of the girls working at the salon. Sylvia noticed that there was one empty space, but fortunately, before she asked the question, she realised that Chantal's photograph had been removed.

When Hans was not around Fred remained cheerful, especially after a few beers. He was convinced that their business was sound and that they were only experiencing teething problems. Everything would turn out fine in the end. If, occasionally, the rent wasn't paid on time, so what! He had other priorities. His family and social life were just as important. Fred and Anita's daughter, Sapphire, was in her late teens and got most of their attention. She had managed to struggle through her basic studies, but was undecided in which direction to go further; nothing that required too much study of course. Maybe she could train as a beauty specialist, or as a model, or hair stylist. There were plenty of training courses advertised in the girly magazines desperately seeking girls like her. It was just a matter of persuading papa to put down the deposit. She was rather a spoilt brat and also prudish. She tended to look down on the work the girls in the salon were doing.

'If I had a daughter like that I would put her in her place,' grumbled Laura, having a problem restraining herself. 'She is a crafty little manipulator if ever I saw one.'

Fred's son Alfred, from his previous marriage, occasionally helped in the salon, he was in his early twenties and independent. He survived well on his own and had a small apartment. He was a friendly character and all the girls liked him He would sometimes pop in to see his parents and chat to the girls at the bar.

Although Anita was good at cooking Indonesian food, it required too much preparation and cooking time, and as she spent most days at the salon she had got into the habit of ordering take-away food. Roy, their friendly restaurant owner became a frequent visitor. Sometimes her son and daughter would join them. Alexandra would shake her head in dismay when rubbish bags, full of empty beer cans and half empty packets of food, were put out for the rubbish collector.

A blast of fresh air blew into the salon. A young and attractive girl called Babs. She had chocolate brown coloured skin, dark eyes and long black hair woven into dreadlocks and decorated with coloured beads. When she smiled she displayed a row of glistening white teeth. She was proud of her curvaceous figure and had a rather pronounced bottom which she accentuated by wearing tight jeans.

She was an instant attraction to the clients and, to the annoyance of the other girls, she also proved irresistible to one or two of their regulars. It was like the lure of an exotic cocktail, when one is on holiday in the sun; it must be tried at least once. Fortunately her massage techniques were far from perfect, and they quickly reverted to their old favourites.

Babs had heard about Body Touch from Chantal, and was filling in time while waiting for a job as Go-Go dancer in a smart night club planned to be opened soon in Amsterdam.

She loved dancing and was convinced that she was would finish up in show business. When nobody objected, she would put one of her own CD's in the HiFi system and turn up the volume. The other girls would watch in fascination as she danced to Reggae music in front of the large mirror, perfecting her body movements and her facial expressions. She was a natural exhibitionist and would swirl around singing to the music. Her dancing was so infectious that the other girls could not resist joining in, following her instructions and clapping their hands. In no time the salon was turned into an aerobics class.

One evening, Roy happened to be delivering take away for the girls during one of these spontaneous dancing sessions. He sat at the bar watching in amazement, until Laura grabbed his arm, gave him a kiss and forced him to join in. He was soon overwhelmed as the only man amongst so many sexily dressed and attractive ladies.

Fortunately Fred and Anita had left early, so they locked the front door and turned up the music. For the rest of the evening it was party time.

'We can't have a party without something to drink,' said Laura, suddenly appearing from behind the bar waving a bottle of Fred's wine. 'Look what I've found.'

She gave the bottle and an opener to Ron, who, like a true connoisseur, first checked the label.

'I wouldn't let this cat's piss near my customers,' he sneered. 'You ladies deserve something better.'

He pulled out his mobile, called his restaurant and ordered two white wines, two red wines and some more Indonesian delicacies.

The next morning Fred frowned in disbelief at the collection of empty bottles, wine glasses, full ashtrays and discarded plastic plates, but was relieved when he checked his stock of wine and beer and found that nothing had been touched.

Hans van der Terp began to take more interest in the running of the business. He would turn up uninvited and sit for hours with Fred in his office trying to help him think up ways of improving the turnover. *Why don't they stay open longer in the evenings? Why don't they install a fruit machine? Why don't they open on the weekend? Could the girls be sent out as masseuses to guests at nearby hotels? How far were the girls prepared to go? Could they use the salon on the weekends for private receptions? Were the premises suitable for couples-evenings, a popular trend in Holland?*

The next step was for Fred to talk to the girls, one by one, to find out their reactions.

Sylvia was the first to be called in. With Fred sitting next to her, Anita tried to explain the situation.

'The business is not doing as well as it should,' she said, with a worried frown on her face. 'The costs are turning out to be higher than expected. One of the main causes, is the rent, it is far too high. We tried to persuade Hans to lower it, but he will not listen. He insists on sticking to the contract. He is just a money grabber. Our only alternative is to find ways of increasing our earnings.'

Fred interrupted. 'You mustn't believe these rumours that Hans is spreading, that we are way behind with the rent. It's not true. From now on we want to keep his nose out of our business, and we hope we can rely on your cooperation.'

Sylvia nodded in agreement. She had never found the man sympathetic, and she felt obliged to show some loyalty to Fred and Anita. But, what were their plans?

'We are trying to find ways of cutting costs and increasing earnings, and any ideas from you ladies would be welcome,' explained Anita. 'One possibility, we are considering, is to give a service to clients at their hotels. Would you be interested?'

'Yes, I wouldn't mind?' Sylvia had been expecting the question. 'But only if it's a respectable hotel that's not too far from here and only if I can agree the program in advance. Also my travelling time and costs would have to be covered.'

'You don't seem to have any problem with men customers.' said Fred, feeling his way cautiously. 'But what do think if we advertise for women clients?'

Sylvia did not answer immediately; her mind was turning at full speed. *What do they expect from me? Don't commit yourself to anything you might regret later.*

'I'm not sure, I have no experience with women,' she answered carefully, 'Maybe I can handle it. Maybe I can't.'

'You don't have to do anything against your will,' Anita said hastily. ʹBut you can learn from experience.ʹ

Sylvia felt uncomfortable. 'I don't have any lesbian or bi-sexual feelings, at all,' she said, getting up to leave.

Anita looked annoyed and Fred looked embarrassed. The discussion was over. Sylvia left the office and returned to her seat next to Alexandria, ignoring her questioning look. They watched as Laura took her turn in the office.

For the rest of the afternoon there was a subdued atmosphere in the salon. Everyone had to face up to reality. If they couldn't solve their problems Fred and Anita would eventually have to close the business.

Later in the evening Fred was back to his old cheerful self. He gave all the girls a drink to put them at their ease, while he explained that, for the time being, the only changes for them would be; that they should put more effort into persuading their clients to order more drinks, and that they should be more flexible with their finishing times if clients turned up late in the evening. In addition he had ordered a fruit machine which would be placed in the corner next to the clothes rack by the front door.

Fred organised a separate drinks cupboard behind the bar, which he stocked up with the more expensive wines, champagne and whisky. It was amusing to see how he would keep the cupboard locked and carry the key around clipped to his belt.

At first the girls were enthusiastic, competing on a friendly basis, to see who could push the highest number of glasses each day. They used all their charms to keep the clients longer at the bar, both before and after their programs, and some even read the sports and financial pages so that they could prolong the conversations. But they soon lost interest when they realised that while being tied up at the bar for a few extra cups of coffee, they were missing opportunities when new clients walked in.

Fred's friend, the pseudo playboy Jamiel, began turning up regularly, mostly on a Friday evening. His flashy clothes, flamboyant manner and cheerful chatter brightened up the bar. He would say till closing time, drinking his beer and chatting to Fred, Anita and the girls. The girls suspected, from Anita's reactions, that he must have been an old flame of hers.

The fruit machine was an attraction Jamiel couldn't resist. His gambling instincts would take over and he would spend hours behind the screen in the corner, with his beer and a pocketful of coins, giving occasional exclamations of joy or dismay.

The girls found him amusing and soon realised that his flirtatious remarks were harmless; he was more talk than action. This was a challenge that Laura who could not resist. An evil glint would appear in her eyes as she sat next to him, whispering teasing remarks in his ear, trying to provoke him into taking a massage. The most she achieved was a glass of wine.

Sometimes Jamiel would bring along business associates, who's main objective was female company. On one occasion he introduced a wealthy associate from Saudi Arabia, a short solidly built man, dressed in a smart business suit. Desperate to make the most of his brief escape from a rigorous society, his large eyes flicked non-stop in the direction of the girls. Eventually he whispered something to Jamiel who in turn whispered the message to Fred.

'He wants a one hour massage with the young blond, and would like to take a bottle of your best champagne with him.'

Fred quickly took Ariella into his office. Ten minutes later they watched as the blond girl went upstairs, like a lamb to the slaughter, followed by her client holding a bottle and two glasses. Jamiel gave her an encouraging gesture suggesting that everything would be O.K.

'Our amateur looks rather nervous,' remarked Laura, with a cynical smile. 'Why doesn't such a guy take someone more experienced?'

'Like you, you mean?' Sylvia was relieved that she hadn't been chosen herself. 'He comes from a different culture. He's probably already got two or three *mature* women like you at home.'

Laura did not appreciate the joke 'Well, if he wants to throw his money away. That's his problem.'

Sensing that an eruption was building up, Fred quickly searched through his box of CD's and fished out an envelope illustrated with a picture of a belly dancer. As he turned up the volume they were all transported to Marrakesh, overwhelmed by an unintelligible, high pitched wailing of a female Arabian singer backed up by strange percussion and stringed instruments playing vibrant and hypnotic music.

Jamiel's eyes filled with nostalgia and Anita swayed to the rhythm. They began to discuss the influence Arabian and Western cultures had on each other. Jamiel nodded in a condescending manner at her misguided theories.

Alexandra watched intrigued. 'What an interesting couple they make. I wonder when Fred is going to be dumped.'

'No chance,' snapped Sylvia. 'She knows there would be no future in such a relationship. She told me once that Jamiel had been dumped by his Dutch wife because he neglected her.'

She felt irritated at Alexandra's comment. Fred had allowed her special privileges. She was allowed to start work later and finish earlier than the other girls. He was happy to have such a classy replacement to Puck who showed no sign of returning.

Just before closing time the Arab suddenly appeared at the bar, fully dressed. He said something to Jamiel and, to everyone's surprise, walked out. Jamiel looking embarrassed, leaned over the bar, said something to Fred, and then followed his friend.

The next morning there was no sign of Ariella, the young blond. When all the girls had arrived Anita called them together to explain what had happened.

'Last night when you had all left, she came into our office in a very upset state. She told us that Jamiel's friend had at first been very friendly and together they had drunk several glasses of champagne. But when she became a bit tipsy he pushed her on to the bed and tried to force himself on her. When she refused he offered her extra money. He wouldn't stop until she threatened to scream. Then he called her a bitch and left. She was so upset we had to give her a lift home.'

'What a bastard,' said Laura, waving her fist. 'Just because they have plenty of money some guys think they can get away with anything. If had he had treated me like that I would have kneed him in the balls.'

'This is the first time we've had a problem like this,' Anita continued, 'I think we should work out a plan of action, in case something similar happens in the future.'

'Why not put an alarm button in each room?' suggested Alexandra.

'And we could do with a bouncer,' laughed Chantal. 'Maybe Fred could learn karate,'

Fred had disappeared in his office to call Jamiel. He considered him to be partly responsible for the loss of a valuable masseuse and he warned him that, in future, he should be more careful what type of business colleague he brought along with him.

Personally Fred did not miss the young blond, he could relate better to more mature ladies. But he was annoyed that he must now find a replacement. Finding suitable girls, especially young ones, was not easy. Anita immediately went into action, adjusting her advertisements and placing them in the sort of publications she hoped would reach interested young ladies.

'It will soon be *black book* time,' said Laura, smiling mischievously.

'What do you mean? What black book? Sylvia was mystified.

'Well, he tries to keep it hidden in his jacket pocket. But once he left it behind the bar and I couldn't resist looking in it. He has a little black book with a list of client's names and telephone numbers'

'What's so special about those clients?' Chantal joined in.

'They are the numbers of guys who prefer variety and want to know when someone new is available. Whenever he takes on a new girl, he disappears in his office for hours calling all the numbers.'

A few days later a young and attractive, lightly coloured girl turned up for an interview. She was obviously of mixed race, partly Antillean, and had traces of negroid ancestry in her features. She had finished her studies and was having a problem finding a suitable job.

After her interview, they watched Fred escort her to the door Laura nudged Sylvia. 'Guess what happens next.'

Fred patted his jacket pocket as he nodded to Anita and disappeared into the office.

'He could do more for us,' complained Chantal. 'It's all very well concentrating on the new girls, but I haven't had a client all morning.'

'That's right, he takes us too much for granted, like old furniture.' Sylvia felt obliged to sympathise with Chantal, although she knew she had nothing to complain about. She had built up a good bond of friendship with Fred an Anita.

She switched her attention to an animated conversation taking place between Laura and Babs. They were discussing, in a rather uninformed manner, the differences and attractions of the major world religions in comparison with trendy new age spiritualism. Babs with her African family origins was obviously trapped in a different time warp, and was under the influence of a more primitive and superstitious pagan religion.

Sylvia realised that Laura and Babs were on completely different wavelengths and was beginning to lose interest when something strange happened. The discussion seemed to have triggered off some deep emotion in Babs. She suddenly seemed to lose control. Her hands were suspended above her knees, her eyes were shut and her lips were trembling.

'She is having problems with her legs,' said Laura, holding Babs hands. 'She is convinced that someone wants to harm her, to weaken her legs so that she can't dance.'

Anita jumped up looking concerned. 'She must be in a trance; it's her subconscious taking over. We have similar phenomena in Indonesia; it's a mixture of fact and fantasy. All we can do is to try to calm her down and distract her. We must put on some calming music and take her to the bar for a cup of tea.'

After ten minutes Babs was back to normal, smiling sheepishly, as though nothing had happened.

The new arrival, Manuela, was in her early twenties and full of energy, like Babs, and was hoping to become a model. Every day she surprised them with a different outfit. One day she would have coloured ribbons in her hair, the next day it was sprayed silver as though she had escaped from a science fiction film set. She would chatter for hour's non-stop with Babs, about make up, breast enlargements, nose adjustments, artificial nails, hair straighteners and various forms of beauty treatment.

Their incessant unintelligent chatter irritated the other girls, especially Alexandra. One afternoon she could stand it no longer and slammed the magazine she was reading down hard on the floor, jumped up and rushed down stairs.

Manuela's chin dropped in surprise. 'What's her problem? She asked, in a slow drawl. 'Is she having a bad day?

'She has more class than you will ever get in your life,' snapped Sylvia.

She guessed that it must be more than the chatter that was upsetting Alexandra and followed her downstairs. She found her collapsed in a chair. Her body was shaking and her face was buried in her hands as she tried to muffle the sound of her sobbing.

Sylvia felt a rush of sympathy. She closed the door, sat next to Alexandra and put her arm round her shoulder. Her friend, the woman she admired so much, was suffering and needed help.

Eventually she calmed down, straightened up and put on a brave face. 'I'm sorry. This is so embarrassing.' she sniffed, wiping her eyes on a towel. 'It's just that I'm going through a bad time at the moment.'

Sylvia realised that it was something more serious than the two ego trippers upstairs that was upsetting her. 'Is it trouble at home? She asked in a sympathetic voice.'

Alexandra put her head in her hands again. 'Yes,' she seemed relieved to be able to talk to someone. 'I thought I could handle it, but we've been together for fifteen years. It's just not possible.'

'Your husband?' It was becoming obvious to Sylvia what the problem was.

'Yes, you wouldn't believe it, he sent me an e-mail. After fifteen years, he sent me an e-mail. He's found someone else, a girl in his office in South America, much younger of course, and he's planning to stay there.' She lifted her head and looked at Sylvia. 'I should have seen it coming I suppose, He travels so much and I know he's had affairs before, but we always managed to patch things up.'

She suddenly straightened up and her expression changed from sorrow to anger. 'The little bitch has told him that she is pregnant and he feels obliged to support her.' She snapped, throwing the towel across the room. 'The idiot, he will be fifty this year and is already past his peak. He is being trapped by a bimbo playing to his ego, flaunting her sexuality to catch what, she imagines is, a wealthy foreigner.'

Sylvia was rather at a loss for words. It all seemed so sudden. 'Well, maybe you are better off without him.' She said softly, trying to give her emotional support.

Alexandra gave her hand a squeeze, 'You're right, life must go on.' She stood up, smoothed her clothes and checked her make-up in the mirror. 'Thanks for your help. I feel better now. Why don't we go back upstairs and have a large whisky?'

The next day Alexandra arrived early, looking relaxed and more glamorous than usual, determined to get on with her life. She spoke to Fred and they disappeared into his office. After ten minutes they were still busy and Laura's curiosity got the better of her. On the pretext of looking for a dropped earring she hovered outside the door eavesdropping on their conversation.

'Just as I thought,' said Laura as she returned and sat down next to Sylvia. 'They are discussing the possibility of her visiting clients outside the salon. I remember Fred once mentioning that he sometimes gets enquiries from business men staying at hotels.'

'Yes I know, I already told him I would be interested in that sort of work,' Sylvia felt disappointed that she hadn't been asked again.

'Me also, it would make a nice change from being stuck in here all day, and with the right client you can earn more, especially if it's on an escort basis for several hours. Anyway, he needs at least two girls for that sort of work, in case one is not available for some reason.

When Alexandra eventually left the office, Laura went and banged on the door with her fists. 'I need to speak to you Fred,' she said in a commanding voice.

'O.K., O.K., calm down,' said Fred, as he reluctantly opened the door. 'Keep it short, I don't have much time.'

106

The following day, in the early evening, it all came out in the open. After receiving a phone call, Fred called Alexandra to the bar and gave her some written instructions. She grabbed her shoulder bag, put on her coat and waved her car keys at the girls as she left. By now everybody knew what was happening.

Although, for the rest of the afternoon, business continued as normal, there was a detectable air of suspense in the atmosphere. When would she return? Would it be a success? Would this become a routine activity for some of the girls?

Fred tried to look unconcerned, but couldn't resist looking at his watch every ten minutes.

Sylvia began to wonder what she was missing. She felt restless. She also needed a new challenge. Once again her fantasies began to take over. She could visualise Alexandra meeting her client at the bar in a smart hotel, their introductory chat with a glass of wine, the bottle of champagne waiting in the hotel room and the erotic arousal as they removed their clothes.

Alexandra returned after about three hour's absence. She had obviously recovered from her emotional upset of the previous day and was looking her normal glamorous self. From the self satisfied look in her eyes it was obvious that she had enjoyed herself.

Although it didn't happen very often, Sylvia couldn't help feeling envious whenever she watched Alexandra or Laura getting prepared and leaving for an adventurous rendezvous.

She felt she was being neglected and decided to follow Laura's example and confront Fred in his office.

She came straight to the point, trying to mimic Laura in one of her aggressive moods. 'When are you going to arrange an interesting trip for me Fred?'

He gave her a strange look. 'I think you are over romanticising this sort of work. You should realise it is not just wining, dining and a massage. Clients normally expect more than a massage. Anyway, you are rather young to send out on your own. You should leave it to the heavyweights.'

So, she thought as she slammed the door behind her, *I'm only a lightweight, only suitable for a massage salon.* She grabbed a magazine, sank into a chair and, for the next few hours, ignored everyone. She even shook her head when Anita offered her a coffee.

Eventually it was too much for Fred.

'Come with me,' he said, grabbing her arm, pulling her into the office and pushing her into a chair. 'Why don't you stop acting like a sulky Prima Donna and face reality? I have enough problems keeping this business going without you telling me what to do. Two of my top ladies have agreed to make external visits and you are getting jealous. Who's going to do the work here if you are all out of the office half the time? I pay for a lot of advertising to attract clients and I need you here. You are our top masseuse and I do my best for you.

He stood up stared into her eyes and extended his hand. 'Do you understand?'

'Yes,' she answered, shaking his hand. 'You are right.'

Sylvia had to face reality and accept that her place was in the massage salon. Fred had made it quite clear that he could not manage without her. But, she began to feel restless and, sometimes, while massaging a client, her thoughts would drift off and she would fantasise about other possibilities.

Alexandra was becoming more and more in demand by her escort clients. She had soon discovered that it was the best way to maintain her luxury life style. Sylvia began to see less and less of her.

Laura was also secretly jealous, as Fred was not organising many assignments for her. She suspected that he turned down some requests, to keep her available for clients in the salon. Behind Fred's back she began to place her own advertisements, using a different name, and suddenly she began to take time off, with the excuse of a head ache or nausea feeling.

Eventually the inevitable happened. Alexandra left. She had found a more sophisticated agency, with a more sophisticated clientele, operating in The Hague. Her absence created a void that was difficult to fill. Sylvia missed her the most, especially as she was always Alexandra's first choice whenever she needed help to keep clients amused at the bar. Also Fred and Anita missed her but did not make it obvious. They were sure that they would eventually find a replacement.

The vitality of the salon began to decline. The wealthier clients, previously attracted by Alexandra, who were always generous with their money, did not appear any more. Babs stayed away, continuing to suffer from pains in her legs. Manuela had no success in finding work as a model, and was becoming moody and sullen. She was losing her popularity. Even Laura was sometimes criticised by clients for being less than enthusiastic.

It became quieter in the salon. Fred was again busy with his misguided economising, cutting down on advertising and buying the cheapest supermarket wine. He spent hours in his office on the telephone.

Irritations grew and tempers became shorter. One evening a group of three boisterous young guys ordered some drinks at the bar and began to make loud remarks about the lukewarm beer. They demanded that Anita fetch some colder beer from the back-up cooler downstairs.

As she was about to leave the bar, Fred stopped Anita with his arm stretched out in front of her.

'Nobody orders my wife around like that,' he said, with a cold look in his eyes. 'If it doesn't suit you here you had better leave.'

'But I just about to take a massage,' complained the biggest man, probably the leader. 'I fancy that blond with the short skirt.' He waved his glass in Laura's direction. 'Hey! Blondie, would you like a drink from me?'

Ignoring the glaring look from Fred, Laura stood up, went to the bar, sat next to the man and began an animated conversation with him and his friends.

Anita raised her hand to her mouth and mumbled, 'How can anyone be so insensitive.'

With a wide grin Laura took a swallow out of the glass that Fred had reluctantly poured out. 'Thank you Fred,' she said, condescendingly. 'This gentleman would like an hour's body-to-body.'

She stood up and led the young man down to the changing room.

When Laura was had disappeared out of site, Fred took her glass and smashed it on the floor.

'Outrageous! What disrespect. Making me look stupid. But she will regret it.'

He slammed the door of his office behind him.

The other two young men at the bar managed to refrain from laughing. Without their leader they behaved themselves, chatting quietly until he had finished his massage.

The next day Laura was called into the office. Nobody knew what was said, but for the following few days she held herself remarkably quiet and only spoke to Fred when it was absolutely necessary.

Sylvia realised she was losing her motivation. Sometimes she massaged her clients in a half hearted manner and did not pay full attention to their stories. She yearned for a change and began to wonder if perhaps she could find more adventure and excitement elsewhere. Her curiosity was aroused when one of her clients told her about a club he had visited, just south of Rotterdam. Apparently it was very luxurious, with a sauna and luxurious rooms, and had a large bar and disco in the reception area. He said it was like going to a non-stop party. The visual image had stuck in her mind.

Life in the salon drifted on like a ship without a rudder. The clientele was falling and as a result the turnover at the bar was also falling. Team work had disappeared and the girls competed hard against each other for the few clients that did turn up. Babs was still sick and had not appeared for weeks.

Out of boredom, during a quiet period, Sylvia began to scan through the personnel required columns, in the erotic sections of the newspapers. One ad caught her eye. A club called Aphrodite, in Breda, was looking for new girls. Suddenly she was wide awake. *That's it! That's the club he told me about.* She felt a rush of excitement, grabbed her mobile and punched in the number.

She was surprised when it was answered by the manager. They needed one or two new girls and if she was suitable she could start the next day.

When she left that evening she told Fred she needed a few days off.

Sylvia was on her way to a new adventure and like the day of her first visit to Body Line she was feeling a mixture of excitement and uncertainty. It was the tail end of summer, and she relaxed and gazed out of the window as the train sped past the built up suburbs of Rotterdam, crossed the majestic waters of the Maas and cruised through the patchwork of fields and villages of South Holland. She smiled to herself as she thought of the empty place on the settee in the salon and the questioning looks it would cause.

She had dressed for the occasion and was wearing a short, sexy black satin dress, with a wide copper coloured belt round her waist, black stockings and black high heeled shoes. Under her dress she was wearing a new maroon and black bra and panty set. She wore a long black leather coat and carried a black leather handbag. Her bag was full of make up and perfume. She was ready for the new challenge.

When she stepped out of the train at Breda station it was like entering a different world. After Rotterdam Central, the world harbour station full of anxious people hurrying in all directions, it was like an oasis of tranquillity. Everyone seemed more relaxed, dressed more casually and with time to move at a more leisurely pace, with time to light a cigarette or browse through the magazines at the kiosk.

As she passed through the exit she raised her hand to shade her eyes from the bright sun and take in the scene before her. A broad boulevard, lined with stately town houses, tall leafy trees and ornate cast iron lantern poles, led to the town centre. The restaurant terraces and snack bars opposite the station were already busy. The inevitable traffic, cars, busses and taxis speeding in all directions, disturbed the peace.

Breda radiated an almost Bourgondisch atmosphere. Sylvia felt the suspense and excitement of a tourist taking her first steps in a strange land. She glanced at her watch. It was twelve thirty. Her appointment was for one-o-clock. She unfolded the notepaper containing the directions she had written down.

'Hey! Young lady, can I help you?' A young man, wearing a bright yellow shirt was waving his arm out of a taxi window, sensing the chance of a fare. He looked the sympathetic type.

She hesitated; there was still time to find a bus or tram. But, *what the heck*, she thought. It can't be too far and at least I will be there on time.

'I'm trying to find this place,' she showed him the address on the notepaper. 'Can you take me there for a reasonable price?'

The young man gave a soft whistle. 'Chic club,' he said looking at her with his eyes wide open. 'Jump in. It's not too far. It will only cost a few Euros.'

He was unable to restrain his curiosity. 'Is this your first day? He asked, as she slid into the back seat.

'Maybe,' she nodded,

The taxi meandered through the old centre of the town, past rows of elegant shops and offices, interspersed with restaurants, terraces and snack bars, full of customers having coffee or lunch. They left the centre and drove along shady lanes flanked by large company and institutional buildings. Gradually the roads became more countrified.

'I hope you aren't making a detour,' joked Sylvia. 'It seems to be further than I imagined.'

'Trust me, madam. I shall get you there in time to catch a handsome rich client,' he said, as he turned his head and winked at her. 'I pick up guys there quite often, but have never been inside. They don't welcome men like me.'

Eventually he turned his taxi into a driveway leading up to a large, spread out building that looked like a smartly converted farmhouse, and stopped by the main entrance.

The young driver looked pleased as she stepped out and paid him the fare plus a tip. As he drove off she went to the door and rang the doorbell that was mounted on a large brightly polished brass plate, embellished with the name *Cub Aphrodite*.

After a few seconds the door was opened by an attractive young blond girl. 'My name is Kim and you must be Sylvia,' she said, as she extended her hand in welcome. 'The boss Adrie is expecting you, please follow me.'

From the entrance hall they passed through what seemed like a labyrinth of passages. She couldn't work out what the original building had been, but guessed that it was a collection of buildings joined together. It smelt stuffy and was rather dark due to the small windows. The walls were clad in a sort of gold coloured material, decorated with erotic pictures, and the floor was covered with dark red carpeting.

Kim walked surprisingly fast on her high heels. Sylvia estimated her age to be in the early twenties, slightly younger than herself. She wore a short black skirt and a rose coloured jumper with deep cleavage, revealing her well endowed bosom.

'He's having his lunch,' she said, as she stopped and opened a door.

They entered what was obviously a kitchen, where a man was sitting at a large wooden table eating from a bowl of pasta. He was in his mid forties but was already grey haired and had a lined face. He was rather corpulent and his grey blue eyes sized her up with a penetrating look.

He put down his fork, but did not stand up. 'You must be Sylvia, the masseuse who has had enough of massage work and is looking for something more exciting.' He spoke with a cynical undertone. 'Well, I can't say if you will like it here, but I will give you the chance to try it out. You can start today, if you like, but you had better stick to the afternoons for a while. At the moment we have enough girls in the evenings.'

He turned to Kim, 'Please show this young lady around the facilities and explain the working arrangements.'

He turned back to Sylvia, 'If you have any questions, just come and ask me. Is everything clear?' He did not smile or give her any encouragement.

'I understand,' she answered. She was not planning to let herself be intimidated by such an authoritarian man.

Again she followed Kim, this time up some wooden stairs, which seemed to be the back way up to the floor above. At the top Kim opened a door and they entered a spacious landing area. As her eyes adjusted to the dim lighting she was amazed to find herself in the heart of a bordello. The floor was covered in a deep plush red carpet, the walls were decorated in gold and silver embossed material and large crystal chandeliers hung from the ceiling. Several polished mahogany doors led off the landing area. Each door was identified by an erotic name in gold letters. At the far end of the area a wide stair way curved down to the ground floor.

'There are five rooms available,' Kim began her introduction. 'They are all similarly furnished. This is where you will entertain your clients.' She pushed open one of the doors.

The room was large and luxuriously furnished, with a cream coloured carpet and softly lit by imitation candle lamps on the walls. The windows were hidden by mushroom coloured drapes held in place by thick gold tasselled cords. An enormous four poster bed was covered with dark maroon satin sheets. A white commode embellished with gold animals and scrolls, and a matching upholstered armchair, stood before a large mirror. On one side of the room a large alcove containing a shower cubicle and a Jacuzzi was partly hidden by heavy curtains.

Kim pointed to the small bedside table. 'The lighting can be dimmed from that little panel on the wall behind the table. There is also a dial for background music and an internal telephone which you can use to order drinks from the bar.' She smiled knowingly. 'Don't forget you also get a percentage.'

Sylvia gazed round the room in amazement. The client would be made to feel that he was in a high class hotel where all his wishes would be fulfilled. She couldn't wait to try out her talents as seductive temptress in such surroundings.

'Naturally we have only the best facilities here and we tend to attract the wealthier clients. Let me show you the price list.'

Kim picked up a red folder, that was standing like a menu card on the commode, and began reading, 'Use of room € 200 per hour, a bottle of champagne € 80.' She replaced the folder. 'You get half the room hire, so the longer you can persuade your client to stay the more you earn.'

'And the rest?' Sylvia had no idea what she should charge for her personal services.

Kim raised her eyebrows. 'You have to negotiate with your client. But, with your looks you will be in demand. I will give you some tips later.' She paused, as she heard the sound of a car entering the driveway, then moved towards the door. 'I shall show you the reception area and bar and introduce you to Archie. 'Let's go.' She was suddenly in a hurry.

Sylvia followed her down the wide curving staircase which opened out into a large, dimly lit, reception area. It was like entering a Greek temple, with a high ornate ceiling supported by white pillars with Venus-like statues at their base. Several alcoves between the pillars were provided with soft upholstered divans and coffee tables decorated with bouquets of flower. At the far end of the room was a large open hearth fireplace.

The entrance was at the left of the stairs partly hidden by a tall sculptured waterfall. On the right under the curve of the stairs was a long copper and brass bar arrangement with a gallery of bottles of, liqueurs, whisky's and brandy's, glistening in candlelight.

116

A tall rather large solidly built man smartly dressed in a black dinner jacket and bow tie was busy polishing glasses behind the bar.

Kim led Sylvia to the bar. 'This is Sylvia,' she said to the man. 'She is starting with us today. Please introduce yourselves.' She began to walk back towards the entrance. 'Sorry! But I think a client is arriving, I must go.' She disappeared through the entrance area.

'Hallo, I'm Archie,' he shook her hand with a strong grip. I'm the barman. I control the use of the rooms and the client payments. I help you with your clients at the bar and give you support when necessary. I advise you to stay my friend.' He winked mischievously. 'I can be quite useful, especially if you have a difficult client.'

'I shall keep it in mind,' Sylvia smiled. She found the man to be sympathetic. 'Where can I find the changing rooms?'

'Oh! Kim was in too much of a hurry, as usual. That girl needs to be taken down a peg. They are through the door at the end of the bar.' He pointed to his right. 'There you will find the lockers, the showers, the toilets, hair dryers and the relaxation area.'

Sylvia was about to go to the changing room when they heard footsteps approaching and voices speaking in English.

Archie pointed to a stool and quickly placed a glass of wine in front of her.

Kim, smiling attentively and chatting like a flirtatious schoolgirl, was hanging on the arm of a tall, attractive, wide shouldered man, who was smartly dressed in a light coloured suit. Walking next to them was an older grey haired man.

'Hello Archie,' the tall man moved Kim's hand away from his arm and approached the bar. He shook Archie's hand enthusiastically. 'It's nice to see you again. You haven't changed a bit.' He spoke with an American accent in strong dark voice.

'You also, Sir. It must be six months ago. What brings you back to our country?'

'Oh! Business as usual.' As he spoke his eyes fixed enquiringly on Sylvia and he sat on the stool next to her.

'This is a nice young lady, is she new here?' He asked Archie.

'Let me introduce you. This is Sylvia. She is a masseuse from Rotterdam. This is her first day.'

The man turned to Sylvia and extended his hand, 'Pleased to meet you, my name is Dan. As you have probably guessed, I am American. I come to

117

Holland once or twice a year for business and always enjoy a visit to this place.' He took hold of her hands and looked at her long sensual fingers. 'I can see you have real massage fingers. How would you like to try out your talents on me later?'

'Of course,' Sylvia was immediately aroused at the idea. She felt an irresistible excitement at the thought of satisfying the sexual demands of such a handsome and experienced man. She knew she was in a different world from Body Touch and was ready for her next naughty adventure.

Kim gave her an angry look and, realising she had lost her advantage, turned her attentions to the older man.

There was a loud pop as, without being asked, Archie opened a bottle of expensive looking champagne and filled some tall slender glasses.

The American nodded in approval. 'Champagne? You remember how I like to get the party going. Don't forget the girls, my friend. We must show our appreciation of the ladies.'

'Yes!' the older man felt obliged to join in. 'Ladies make life worth living.' He was more than happy with the attentions of Kim.

Archie turned up the music and the atmosphere became more relaxed as they raised their glasses and toasted each other. As Dan spoke to Archie it became apparent that he was quite wealthy and owned two night clubs in Philadelphia.

They finished the bottle of champagne and chatted casually about the weather, travel and sport. Sylvia contributed some witty remarks in her almost perfect English.

'Not only beautiful, but intelligent as well,' said Dan, in genuine admiration. 'I could earn a fortune with a few girls like you back home.'

The underlying erotic tension was building up and after a few minutes Dan could no longer restrain himself. He put his arm round Sylvia's waist and spoke softly in her ear. 'It's relaxation time. Shall we go upstairs and get to know each other better.'

As they left the bar Archie told her which room she could use and gave her the key, at the same time giving her an encouraging smile. He indicated, by rubbing his finger and thumb together, that he was a good tipper. Sylvia nodded.

As they entered the room Sylvia went to the control panel, turned on the music and dimmed the lights.

'Why don't we start with the Jacuzzi?' she suggested, as she removed her dress.

His eyes almost popped out; he could hardly believe his luck, as she stood before him in her sexy underwear, black stocking and high heels

'Good idea,' he spluttered, almost nervously. 'We have plenty of time and I don't like to rush things.'

She turned on the water in the Jacuzzi, adjusted the temperature and poured in a phial of aromatic oil. While it was filling she laid out some bath towels.

'Let's see how good you are with those erotic fingers,' he murmured as he lowered himself into the warm bubbling water.

She kept him waiting, performing an erotic striptease as she kicked off her shoes and slowly removed her underwear. She couldn't help noticing that he was fully aroused as she lowered herself into the opposite side of the Jacuzzi and began to fondle his toes. Then she began to massage his feet and legs. He gave a contented groan and shut his eyes. She slowly moved closer on her knees, straddling his legs. She leaned forward and began to massage his neck and shoulders. She tried to avoid bodily contact with his penis, which was large and erect. He was getting excited and put his arms round her back and pressed her closer. She kissed him gently on the lips. He was suddenly wide awake and began kissing her passionately. His hands moved onto her breasts and began fondling her nipples, then one hand moved down between her legs and he began playing expertly with her pussy. She felt the wetness as his fingers entered inside her. She did not resist and was almost overwhelmed by a powerful erotic feeling, an irresistible urge to lower herself on to the stiff rod a few centimetres below.

But, he was still in control. 'Not too fast, we are just beginning and I'd like to get to know you better.' He pushed her gently back onto his legs. 'Also I'd like to give you some advice, how to keep your boss happy. In places like this you should push the drinks. Why don't you call the bar and order some more champagne, then we can relax here for half an hour.'

Sylvia stepped out of the Jacuzzi, wrapped a bath towel round her body, picked up the phone by the bed and called Archie.

"It's on the way,' Archie sounded cheerful. 'Don't forget to take your time. Remember, more time more money.'

She returned to the Jacuzzi and lay next to Dan in close body contact. 'Now we can try out those sexy fingers,' he said, guiding her hand down between his legs.

While they chatted casually about superficial subjects her fingers encircled his weapon and she began the sensual caressing techniques she had perfected at Body Line.

After a few minutes there was a gentle knock on the door and Archie entered with a tray containing a champagne bucket and two glasses. He moved discretely, placing the tray by the Jacuzzi. He quickly popped open the bottle and filled the two glasses.

'You might like to know that your colleague Rob is busy with Kim in the next room.' He said to Dan, as he left the room. 'Enjoy yourselves.

'This is the best way to taste champagne,' said Dan, as he put his fingers in one of the glasses, sprinkled some champagne over her nipples and began to lick them with his tongue.

'And this is even better.' His strong hands guided her into position so that she was sitting on his legs facing him. He then gently pushed her top half backwards, pulled her bottom half up onto his stomach and eased her legs apart.

She felt a flash of embarrassment at being trapped in such a vulnerable position, but quickly relaxed when she felt a pleasant tingling sensation as more champagne trickled down between her legs. She felt the thrill of being completely at his mercy and instinctively opened her legs wider, in encouragement, as he moved his head forward and went to work with his tongue.

She entered a world of erotic fantasy as his tongue moved, in circles, up and down, pressing inside, fast and slow. She had never had such an experience. She was completely lubricated when his fingers eventually slid easily inside. He kept up the treatment until he realised from her body movements and moaning noises that she was about to climax.

'That was sensational,' he gasped, raising his head. 'But we have to slow down; we still have plenty of time. The best is yet to come. Let's have some more champagne.' He smiled and waved his glass. 'I haven't drunk much of mine yet.'

Sylvia, resenting the sudden let down, got out of the Jacuzzi and grabbed the towels. She quickly recovered her composure and they playfully dried each other off. *I'll get my revenge* she was thinking.

'Let's try out the bed.' She giggled, as she ran to the bed jumped on top and sprang up and down several times, like a playful child. Then she calmed down and refilled the glasses as he joined her, on his back, in the middle of the bed. They gulped down some more champagne while she moved above him.

'Now it's your turn,' she said teasingly, holding the glass above his penis.

'Go ahead,' he chuckled as she tilted her glass. 'We should call this *champagne sex*. I shall put it on the menu at one of my clubs.'

She sat on his legs, bent her head down and began to lick the liquid off his tummy and then off the side of his erect pole. She was amazed at the stiffness as she fondled it with her fingers. She was still in a teasing mood and was going to get her revenge for him stopping her climax. She moved her hands up and down, faster and faster, and at the same time put her mouth over the top. She was going to push him to the limit. She forced it deep in her mouth, deep in her throat, in and out, sucking hard, until he nearly exploded.

'Stop! Stop!' He was breathing heavily. 'What are you doing to me? I'm loosing control. It's too fast.'

She raised her head, and with an evil grin on her face, got off the bed, turned up the music, put on her high heels and began to dance sensually to the music. Archie's words still echoing in her mind; '*more time more money.*'

Dan sat on the side of the bed, poured out the remaining champagne and enjoyed the show.

She danced teasingly getting closer and closer, until he became desperate, grabbed her hand, pulled her close and threw on the bed. He lifted her bottom with one hand and pressed a cushion under it with the other.

Her legs opened wide as he began to warm her up again with his tongue. But only briefly this time, he was desperate for the real thing. She was wide open and willing, but still felt slightly apprehensive as she watched him move into position with his enormous weapon poised for entry.

He leaned forward, put his hands on her knees and carefully pushed his penis inside. He moved slowly at first until he sensed her lubrication beginning to flow. In and out, deeper and deeper. Every second to be enjoyed. He paused deep inside her and fondled her breasts. She put her arms round him and tickled him gently on his back, then she pressed hard, pulling him into her, and at the same time, moving her long slender legs up high until her toes were behind his neck.

They were both anticipating a prolonged and powerful sexual experience. But there was a sensual competitive element arising between them. Who was the best performer? Who would be the first to lose control?

He was determined to demonstrate his sexual prowess. This would be an experience she would never forget. He had the biggest and the best. He varied his movements, pushing harder and harder, faster and faster. She must be overwhelmed.

She found it exhilarating to be dominated by such an expert. The longer he took and the harder he attacked the more aroused she became. She was amazed at her own capacity and played on his macho image. When he began to slow down she gave him encouragement. 'What a tiger. You're the best I've ever had. How can you keep it up so long?' Each time he responded to the challenge.

At last, remembering Archie's words, she pretended she needed a break in the activities.

'Why don't we have a rest, then I can go on top?'

It was the excuse he needed and he flopped on his back alongside her. After a few minutes she took it firmly in her hands and she moved into position above him. Again she couldn't resist a little sadistic teasing, by taking her time. In a few centimetres, then out. Then in again, then out. She became incredibly juicy and he groaned in desperation, until she lowered her body, and he entered her completely. For the next twenty minutes she used all her tricks and moved as if she was riding a frisky race horse. Occasionally she would stop, give him some erotic hand treatment and then ease it in again. Eventually she realised that being on top meant doing most of the work, and rolled off onto her back alongside him. As they lay still for a few minutes, she fantasised about her performance; *this may be animal lust, but it is amazingly enjoyable.*

'Now its time for me to finish you off?' he said, fondling her breasts. 'This time I want to take you from behind, so that I can stay in control.'

She turned onto her knees; put her chin on her hands, her bottom up high and her knees wide apart. This was the ultimate *'Fuck me'* position. An invitation no man could refuse.

It was his turn to tease her, and he began to play, easing his fingers into her pussy. In this position she was completely vulnerable and could not see what he was doing. *Is that one, two, three or four fingers? Is he trying to get his whole hand in?*

'Go easy,' she said. 'I prefer to feel the real thing.'

He gave her a stinging slap on her bottom, put his hands on her shoulders and, with one quick push, was inside. He began slowly with deep gentle thrusts. An incredible warm sensual feeling began to flow through her body. She felt waves of erotic energy as he slowly built up to a powerful rhythm. She instinctively joined in, coordinating her movements with his, forcing it deep inside; until together they reached an explosive climax. She felt her vaginal muscles gripping and squeezing his pulsating penis, forcing his spurts of liquid deep into her body.

For a few seconds they stayed locked together. Then drifted back to reality and collapsed in each others arms, unable to speak.

After they had recovered and showered together, they returned to the bar, where Archie was chatting to Dan's friend Rob and Kim. A few other sexily dressed ladies had turned up and were meandering around in anticipation of a busy evening.

'Were you trying to break the record?' asked Archie with a cheeky smile. 'Your pal here was finished an hour ago.'

'She's one in a million,' answered Dan, taking hold of Sylvia's hand. 'That was the experience of a lifetime and I had to make the most of it'

'How about a little drink to help you recover?' Archie reached for a bottle of Bourbon whisky.

Dan slapped his hand on top of the bar. 'Good idea, that's what I need. We must keep the party going. Don't forget Rob and the ladies, and something for yourself.' He put his arm round Sylvia's shoulder and kissed her on the cheek.

The two men were in no hurry to leave, preferring to chat to Archie and the girls and to down a few more drinks. Archie was an expert at keeping the conversation going and winked at the girls as he surreptitiously poured them alcohol free drinks, knowing that they must keep sober and attractive for possible further clients.

Kim raised her glass in Sylvia's direction. 'You're doing well on your first day,' she said, at the same time pursing her lips and nodding her head. She realised that the newcomer was going to be a tough competitor.

Eventually it was time for Dan and Rob to leave. They settled their bill and Archie ordered a taxi. They were a little unsteady on their feet as the girls accompanied them to the door. After some farewell cuddles Dan pressed something into each of their hands.

Back at the bar Archie complimented them on their performance. 'They are valuable clients and you both did a great job. I will give you your share before you leave and I hope they gave you a little extra?'

Archie gave a low whistle as they opened their hands and each displayed a one hundred euro note.

It was late afternoon and Sylvia's time was up. She collected her coat and Archie called for another taxi. While she waited at the bar, she felt a warm glow flowing through her body and was relieved that, today at least, she was not obliged to entertain more clients. She watched in amusement as Kim sat further along the bar, chatting up her next victim.

Walking out to the taxi she began to feel slightly weak at the knees. The drinks were taking their effect. The bright low sun flashed through the trees and almost blinded her. She had a strange schizophrenic feeling. Had it all really happened to her? Or had it all been dream? The effect was accentuated as she approached the taxi and was surprised to see the same face, the same yellow shirt and the same hand waving out of the window.

As he helped her into the back of the taxi the young driver couldn't hide his curiosity; 'Did you have a nice time? Did you find a rich client?'

'That's my business,' she said coolly, finding his questions too personal.

'Sorry madam,' he said apologetically. 'I didn't mean any offence,'

As they swept out of the drive she relaxed into her seat and began to think over the events that had taken place. She shut her eyes and mentally calculated the amount she had earned. It tallied with the amount she had received. At first she was satisfied, but then she realised that if she deducted her tip and the train and taxi costs, it was not so very much. Especially if she related it to the total hours involved, between leaving home at ten o clock in the morning and probably reaching home at seven o clock in the evening. She would need three or four clients a day to make it really worth while, and she knew they wouldn't all be as much fun as Dan.

That night her sleep was disturbed by vivid images, as she relived her experiences in her dreams. She heard the popping of champagne corks and a booming voice with an American accent, repeating; *'Beautiful girl. Smart girl'*, She saw the grinning face of Archie as he poured drink after drink, the doting face of Ron as he laughed at his boss's witty remarks and the mixture of envy and encouragement in Kim's eyes. She felt trapped on an

124

enormous bed, unable to escape from a multitude of hands grabbing her naked body.

The next morning she woke early. The birds twittering in the trees outside her window brought her back to reality. Her bed was a riot of sheets and blankets. Her throat was dry and she still felt unsteady as she went to the bathroom and looked in the mirror to assess the damage. Her hair was a mess, she had reddish marks on her face and her eyes were swollen. She quickly swallowed two Paracetemols in a glass of water and spread some moisturiser cream over her face. She fetched two ice cubes out of the refrigerator, wrapped them in a flannel and held them under her eyes, then went back to bed to recover.

'What will be in store for me today?' She thought, as she took a shower, then fixed her hair and carefully applied her make-up. This time, for travelling, she decided to wear some casual clothes, putting on a jumper and jeans. She carefully selected her working outfit for the day; a sexy short red dress covered in sequins and some matching underwear, and put them in her bag together with a pair of red, high heeled, slip-on shoes.

Sylvia was ready for her next adventure.

For the second time she took the train to Breda and then a taxi to the club. Fortunately this time the driver was uninterested and kept quiet. She felt more self assured as she approached the club building, entered a side door, which was already open, and found her way to the kitchen. The grey haired manager was again busy preparing himself some food. She wondered if he spent all his time eating.

He glanced at her and continued with his activities. 'Glad to see you Sylvia. Kim has just called in sick. She worked till late yesterday evening and probably had too much to drink. So you had better quickly go and change and report to Archie, in case any clients turn up.'

She rushed to the changing room, put on her sexy red dress and red high heels, touched up her make-up and sprayed some perfume over her hair.

Archie was alone, behind the bar rearranging some glasses and bottles. 'Good morning,' he said, with a bright smile. 'I like the red outfit. It's quiet at the moment, so why don't you take a seat and read the newspaper while I make you a coffee.'

Sylvia was glad of the chance to relax and catch up with the day's news. But after a few minutes, they were both jolted out of their lethargy. A tall glamorous girl, with long blond hair strode through the door; she had a beautiful, sunburned face and was dressed in a stylish cream coloured outfit with light brown high heeled boots.

'Remember me? She said, in a loud cheerful voice, throwing her bag on a stool and leaning over the bar to give Archie a big kiss.

'Katie!' Archie beamed with surprise. 'How could I forget? It must be at least six months. It's wonderful to see you again.' He turned to Sylvia. 'May I introduce you? This is Katie, our Katie from Scotland. She turns up at least once a year. I believe she has visited all the top clubs in Europe, but she always comes back to us.'

'Pleased to meet you,' said Sylvia, shaking her hand.

'What are you doing here?' continued Archie. 'I thought you were enjoying yourself in the French high society?'

'Oh! Archie! She put on a posh theatrical voice and waved her hand dramatically in the air. 'You wouldn't believe it. I was forced to flee from France. You remember the Marquis and his visits here?'

'Of course. He was crazy about you. I told you to grab your chance and marry him.'

'Well! I was tempted, and it almost happened.' She glanced sideways at Sylvia, realising she was exposing her secrets to a stranger, but continued undeterred.

'I went to stay at his chateau, in Bordeaux, and was seriously weighing up the pros and cons of accepting his proposal, until, one evening, this strange guy burst into my bedroom. He was dressed in fencing gear and began to threaten me. He pranced around waving a sabre under my nose. Then he hissed through his mask, in broken English *'If yu no leef heer, ay weel kot yu op in leetle biits.'*

Apparently my future consort had forgotten to tell me he already had a partner, a jealous boyfriend.'

Both Archie and Sylvia burst out laughing.

'Who would have thought that the Marquis liked his bread buttered on both sides?' joked Archie. 'Really Katie, your life should be turned into a film. I hope you didn't completely waste your time.'

'C'est la vie.' She laughed waving her left hand, displaying a large diamond ring. 'Anyway, his chateau was rather small, and so was he. He didn't like me wearing high heels and he was not a very good performer either, but he was generous while it lasted.'

'So what's your plan now? Are you going to stay with us for a while?' asked Archie.

'That's my intention, for a few months. But, I'm not so young anymore and I hope to go to Australia by the end of the year.'

'Why Australia?'

'Well, I still have contacts in Scotland and I want to start a business selling Scottish sweaters. I managed to sell several while I was in France.'

'So why didn't you start your business in France?' sighed Archie. 'The mother land of fashion.'

'It's always been my dream to go to Australia, and of course, they speak English there………...' Katie did not finish the sentence. She had spotted a good looking young man at the entrance looking around sheepishly. She immediately made a bee-line for him, took his arm and led him into one of the alcoves.

Sylvia watched in amazement, realising she had been slow to react 'What a professional.' She murmured.

'A charming lady,' Archie spoke with admiration. 'Such a lady is worth gold in a club like this.' He leaned on the bar closer to her. 'It's difficult to imagine, but she left Scotland when she was seventeen. She came from a poor family, and has been working on her own in top quality clubs in Europe for the last fifteen years, trying to build up some capital. She has had several rich admirers but always remains a free agent. It's quite a challenge to catch such an exotic bird.'

'Does she have to find somewhere to stay?' asked Sylvia.

'No she likes to use one of the intern rooms we provide for the girls. It allows her to work long hours without relying on public transport to get home late at night. Many of our best clients tend to turn up late in the evening.'

Suddenly, for some reason, he stopped their conversation and moved away from her on the pretext of organising his paperwork. The club suddenly seemed rather impersonal. Then she noticed a man wearing sunglasses sitting alone in one of the alcoves.

She moved closer to Archie. 'You could have told me that a client was here,' she said, feeling annoyed.

'That is not a client.' He answered, keeping his distance. 'That is the club owner. He often turns up unannounced to keep an eye on us. Today he is probably watching you.'

'Why.'

'He checks the accounts every day. He knows you had a wealthy client yesterday and thinks the drinks consumption could have been better.'

Sylvia remembered Dan's advice. *'To keep your boss happy in places like this you have to push the drinks.'*

'Do I have to carry a keg of brandy round my neck like a St Bernard dog in the Swiss Alps?'

'You just have to push the expensive drinks.' Archie spoke coolly.

She was surprised at the sudden change in his character, and decided to stay at the bar and keep quiet. Her pleasure in this adventure was disappearing fast. She felt she was being watched and under pressure.

Almost an hour went by before the next client arrived. A man in his mid forties, with greying hair and dressed in a well worn grey suit. He took a seat at the end of the bar and looked furtively at Sylvia. After a few minutes he said something to Archie who, waved his hand, indicating that she should join them. He immediately poured out two glasses of champagne.

The man was rather nervous and hardly spoke as they finished their drinks. He leaned forward towards Archie.

'May I have half an hour with this lady?' he asked, assuming that Archie made all the decisions.

Sylvia felt, slightly indignant, as if she had no choice in the matter, as though she was a piece of merchandise on display in a supermarket.

'Of course,' answered Archie. He winked as he gave Sylvia the key. 'Why don't you take the rest of the bottle with you?'

The man in grey followed her upstairs, where they both took a quick shower and went directly to the bed.

The man was rather skinny, with white skin. He seemed to be shivering, either from the shower, or from embarrassment. She felt slightly sympathetic and kissed him on his cheek. He reacted immediately, as though he had been given a green light to proceed. Without any finesse he kissed her passionately on the lips. He seemed to have no idea how to relate to ladies.

'You are my friend,' he whispered in her ear. 'From the moment I first saw you.' Then, without asking permission and without any preliminary warming up, he tried to force his hand between her legs.

She kept her legs tightly closed and pushed him onto his back. She was determined to slow him down, but at the same time realised that as a client he was entitled to get his money's worth and satisfy his desires.

'Don't be in such a rush, just relax and let me do the work.'

She moved above him and let him fondle her breasts and kiss her nipples, but she did not feel any sense of arousal. She eased back and held his penis, but it was only half stiff. She tried a few of her erotic movements but there was still no reaction.

'I would rather have a massage,' he said, turning on his tummy, in an effort to cover up his obvious lack of virility. 'I'm tired and I don't know why I came here.'

Sylvia felt obliged to continue and massaged his neck and shoulders. She lowered her breasts, moved them up and down over his back and then down on to his buttocks.

'Don't do that, I don't like it,' he grunted, turning round onto his back. Then he sat up and got off the bed.

'Sorry young lady. This is just not working. I'm obviously not cut out for this sort of entertainment.'

He dressed quickly and got out his wallet.

'Here, this should be enough.' He threw a fifty euro note on the bed. 'I'm not sure if it was worth it.'

He rushed out and slammed the door.

Sylvia was speechless, but also relieved that she had escaped her obligations.

'That was an episode that I prefer to forget.' She thought, as she tidied up the room.

'That man didn't seem too satisfied when he left,' remarked the all seeing Archie, when she returned to the bar.

'I did my best, but he is not the type for this sort of place. He seemed to be suffering from guilt feelings.'

'He is probably rushing home to his wife, right now,' laughed Archie. 'Hopefully we won't see him again.'

The man with the sunglasses was still sitting in the alcove, drinking a whisky. Sylvia turned her back on him, opened her bag and checked her make-up.

'Can I help you sir?' Archie's voice disturbed her thoughts.

She turned to see a rather large, sturdily built, youngish man, with a sheepish grin on his face, approaching the bar. She now knew the routine, and went to join him.

'You must be new here, I haven't seen you before.' He said, looking at her with eyes that were stripping her naked. 'My name is Sjors. I'm an international lorry driver and come here sometimes for relaxation.'

Sylvia suddenly got a sinking feeling in her stomach. It is not only sophisticated, wealthy business men that come here after all. Even truck drivers earn enough to indulge themselves sometimes. She was now expected to satisfy the animal needs of a randy truck driver. What had she let herself in for?

'Would you like something to drink?' asked Archie, reaching for a bottle of champagne.

'Yes, but not that rubbish. I'm thirsty. Give me a real drink. I like German beer.'

He had a simple sense of humour and began telling the latest jokes he'd heard from his buddies on the road. They were mostly about women as sex objects or about mother in-laws. Sylvia laughed half heartedly at his humour.

Archie also had a large repertoire of jokes and he was an expert at selecting jokes that suited the character he was dealing with.

'This is not the reason I'm here,' said Sjors, plonking his empty glass on the table.

A large strong hand gave her a little slap on her knee. 'Come on Darling, let's go upstairs. You're making me incredibly horny.'

Archie found the situation incredibly amusing. He raised his arm and shook his clenched fist as he gave her the key.

She felt she was being handled like a lust object. But something strange was happening, her primitive instincts were taking over. She was beginning to get excited at the idea of submitting to such an oversexed steer.

Once the door was closed there was no turning back. She turned the lights down low to increase the intimacy, and they both quickly removed their clothes. After they had both showered he helped her dry off., and she could not help admiring his figure. He was proud of his build and posed like a body-builder. His weapon was sticking out like a flag pole. Then in one move he swept her up in his arms and carried her to the bed.

He lay on his back and guided her over him until her legs were straddling his face. She offered no resistance and, as his tongue began its work, she felt an erotic tingling sensation spreading through her body. The longer he played the more aroused she became. She felt his fingers entering and moving in and out. She felt her lubrication flowing and instinctively moved her legs further apart in encouragement, as a wave of erotic pleasure engulfed her. Sensing her arousal he continued his movements, faster and faster, until she completely lost control, giving in to a spontaneous spasm that surged through her pussy. She was engulfed in an unstoppable orgasm and was astonished to feel the man's tongue moving eagerly, as her juices flowed into his mouth.

He still had not had enough. He turned her round on top of him and pushed her down while he played with her pussy from behind. She knew what he was hoping for, and bent down to give him some oral treatment. She was fascinated by its size and her fingers seemed small and delicate as they encircled it and moved up and down. This was a challenge she could not resist, and she took a deep breath, opened her mouth and moved it down over the top. She was surprised how much she could manage to get in. The man was overwhelmed and began to move it up and down forcing it in and out.

'What a hot lady,' he said, as she collapsed on the bed next to him.

He leaned over, picked up a condom from the bedside table, ripped open the packing and expertly rolled it into place.

'Now we are ready for the real thing. You are warmed up and it's my turn. I'm going to fuck you until you beg for mercy.'

He lifted her legs up high and wide, and paused for a few seconds to enjoy the sight of a juicy, inviting pussy, ready and waiting. Then he penetrated her slowly, centimetre by centimetre, in and out, and stopped when he was completely inside.

She groaned. 'Don't stop! Fuck me! Fuck me hard!' She put her hands on his shoulders and forced him further into her.

For the next half hour she was in fantasy world, as he attacked her from all directions; on top, from behind, underneath. Whenever he got close to losing control he would pause, calm down and then begin again. She had never experienced such prolonged hard sex.

'This can go on for hours,' she thought. *'Time to take charge and finish him off.'*

She moved on top of him and he was only too happy to lay back and enjoy the treatment. He was still amazingly stiff and she realised it was going to be a challenge to finish him off. She was also still aroused and began to tease him, to make him desperate, by guiding him very slowly in and out of her juicy pussy. Then she let loose with all her tricks. Varying her body movements and her tempo, to wind him up to a peak, but this time she did not ease up when he was reaching a climax.

'I can't hold it any longer,' he moaned, as she moved faster and faster. 'Don't stop. Don't stop.'

She couldn't help getting a slight sadistic feeling, looking into his eyes as she relentlessly bounced up and down, forcing him into an unstoppable climax. His body jerked violently for a few seconds and they collapsed in each others arms.

They were both clammy from sweating and took a shower together. As they chatted she found him to be a pleasant but rather basic character.

'You could give someone a heart attack,' he joked, putting his hand on his chest. 'But what a great way to go.'

Back at the bar, out of politeness, he ordered another German beer for himself and a glass of wine for her. But it was obvious he was losing interest. After a few minutes he asked Archie for some small change, picked up his beer and moved to the fruit machine in an alcove on the far side of the room.

No other customers were waiting and the man with the sunglasses had disappeared. Sylvia was glad of the chance to relax. Her thoughts were drifting back over what had just taken place, when suddenly she heard Katie's voice.

'Hallo, remember me?'

Sylvia turned, to see Katie rushing over to Sjors and giving him a kiss. He was obviously an old client of hers and she was not going to miss the opportunity to make contact again. For a while she joined in his game, feeding coins into the machine while he pulled the lever. Then to Sylvia's amazement she took his arm and led him back upstairs.

She felt insulted. Even though she considered herself socially superior, she had done her best to satisfy the man. Now she could not help visualising him doing the same things with Katie.

'So what! she thought. *'He is a client after all. It's his money and he can do what he likes.'* She looked at the clock. She wanted to go home. But she must stay another half hour.

Then the sunglasses returned and she felt uncomfortable again. She had had enough. She went to Archie.

'I'm leaving early.'

Archie looked surprised. 'What's the problem? You're doing great.' He glanced at the sunglasses. 'The boss won't be too happy. The other girls haven't turned up yet.'

'I have a headache from yesterday.' Her voice was trembling. 'That man with the sunglasses is making me crazy.'

'You shouldn't let him bother you.' Archie was getting annoyed. 'You better go and explain to the manager.'

She went to the locker room, changed her clothes, walked out the back entrance and found her way to the nearest bus stop.

Sitting in the train back to Rotterdam she decided her little escapade in Breda was over, she was never going back. She calmed down and, as she looked around at the other passengers, she began to smile to herself, *'If only they knew what a naughty and exciting time I have had.'*

Later that evening Fred called her on her mobile, to ask if she was fit enough to return to work. He sounded desperate. Babs was still sick, and without Alexandra they were trying to survive with only three girls, Laura, Chantal and Manuela. She was relieved that he apparently had no suspicions about her activities in Breda, and she began to look forward to returning to the salon.

The next day Sylvia returned to Body Touch. Fred, Anita and the girls were all glad to see her back, and she felt relaxed in the old familiar surroundings. She was soon reminded of her popularity when, within a few hours, two of her regulars turned up. She massaged them enthusiastically while they chatted like old friends. She was in control again.

Later, during her lunch break, she had time to relax and to reflect over her wild adventure. She felt frustrated that she had to keep the story to herself. She would have loved to share her experiences with one or more of the other girls, but knew that to do so could spoil her reputation.

She still felt sensually aroused as she re-enacted in her mind the various scenes that had taken place. She had used her female charms, her sexuality and her body, to entice, arouse and satisfy the erotic demands of frustrated men. She felt a sense of achievement; she had broken through all barriers. She had satisfied her curiosity and had played the part of a whore in a high class brothel. She had especially enjoyed her session with the American, but she knew he was an exception and she was glad she had only stayed two days.

Suddenly, her daydreaming was disturbed. The door opened and a dark young lady walked in.

Laura leapt to her feet and rushed to meet her. 'Babs! How are you? Where have you been? What happened to you?

'Am I glad to see you all again,' she said in an emotional voice, at the same tune brushing some tears away. 'I've had such a terrible time. For several days I couldn't walk and had to stay in bed.'

'Did you see a doctor?' asked Laura looking concerned.

'Yes, of course. The doctor sent me to hospital for a check-up but they couldn't find anything. He gave me some pills for the pain and to help me sleep.'

'What was the problem then?' Anita asked, in an unsympathetic voice. 'You could have called us and kept us informed. Do you realise how many of your regular clients have been enquiring about you?'

Babs looked at Anita as if she was about to explain. Then her face tightened up, in reaction to her abrupt manner.

'I'm recovered. That's the only thing that matters. Is my white dress still in my locker?'

'Of course,' snapped Anita. 'Of course it's still there. What else did you expect?'

'Oh! Good, I must change' Babs had found an excuse to escape further questions and went quickly downstairs to the changing room.

'Strange girl,' said Anita. 'I don't think I will ever understand her.'

There were now more than enough girls in the salon and, fortunately, enough clients turned up to keep them all reasonably occupied. Babs was also chosen a few times and was soon back to her old vibrant self. Later in the afternoon, after they had eaten their food and were enjoying coffee, she could no longer contain herself and they all listened in amazement as she told her story.

She explained that she stopped turning up at Body Touch when the pain in her legs began to get worse. They were especially sensitive at night, when they felt like they were burning. As the doctor could not find anything wrong she instinctively began to suspect that someone was having evil thoughts about her and was trying to harm her. She couldn't imagine who it could be. She lived in a large old house with several members of their extended family and they all lived together like one big happy family.

She began to observe everyone more intently, until one day she noticed a self satisfied look on the face of an old aunt, who had recently joined them from Jamaica, when she was telling her that she had to stop her dancing lessons. The look was very brief, but she sensed immediately that there was an element of evil in it. She had been given a glimpse of a primitive force, a darkness of which she had no knowledge. She began to spy on her aunt. She noticed that she knew a lot about spices and herbs, and that she sometimes put something in the tea pot to enhance the aroma.

Her aunt pretended to be friendly towards her, but she didn't trust her any more. Her younger sister told her that the old crone was jealous of her and that she had been persuaded to leave Jamaica because of her dabbling in the occult.

She tried to discuss her suspicions with her mother, but she was reluctant to offend one of her family. 'When you earn enough to live on your own you won't have to see her any more.' She said, as though that would be the answer to the problem.

The pain in her legs continued, until one night when she could not bear the weight of the sheets and blankets on her legs, they finished up on the floor. In desperation she lifted up the mattress and was trying to tuck the sheets back in place, when a photo fluttered down on to the floor. When she picked it up she was amazed to see that it was a photo of her in a bikini. When she looked closer she noticed that small holes had been pricked through the photo, through her legs. She panicked and rushed downstairs screaming, waking every body in the house.

The whole family gathered in the living room trying to calm her down. She waved the photo and pointed at her aunt.

At first her aunt denied everything, but the others forcibly searched the old black handbag she carried everywhere with her, and found more photos of Babs. She suddenly became aggressive, began to curse everybody and rushed up to her room in a hysterical state.

She was no longer welcome and the next day arrangements were quickly made for her return to Jamaica.

'Incredible,' said Fred who had been listening from behind the bar. 'I've heard about things like that happening in Indonesia, but never before in Holland,'

Babs story kept the ladies interested for days. It seemed to stir up their latent primitive superstitions. Suddenly they were all recalling incidents of strange occurrences, mysterious happenings or paranormal experiences.

Even Hans van der Terp, when he heard about Babs experience, appeared to be very concerned. He turned up frequently to comfort her in a fatherly manner.

Much to the fury of Chantal, who looked like she could also prick pinholes in a photo of Babs. 'Massages also seem to be part of the fatherly treatment,' she said sarcastically, out loud.

Hans ignored the remark; he was having too much fun with Babs, who had completely forgotten all her problems. She looked ravishing and was making the most of his attentions.

One evening Hans was in the mood for celebrating and, without asking permission from Fred, called Paddy, an Estate Agent friend of his to come and join him for a few drinks.

Paddy arrived early in the evening and joined Hans at the bar. He was a large solidly built man who could pack away many beers with little apparent effect. Hans was drinking Bacardi and Cola and was keeping

Babs' glass topped up from a bottle of Rosé. Fred looked on with leaden eyes as he provided the dinks, obviously wondering who was going to pay for them.

The more they drank the more frivolous they became, with the men telling risqué jokes and Babs giggling at their every remark. Sometimes Hans couldn't resist making denigrating remarks about the running of the saloon ---- 'What we need is a good publicity agent to bring in the customers.' ---- 'When are we going to get some really cold beer?'

After a few more drinks, both men began kissing Babs, and she did not resist when hands disappeared under her blouse or moved up inside her skirt.

Anita looked on uneasily from the settee. 'They are going too far. They are making Fred crazy.'

Sylvia realized something had to be done. She jumped up and went to the office. A few minutes later she put her head out of the door. 'Babs,' she called in a loud voice. 'Telephone for you.'

Babs almost stumbled as she stood up, steadied herself and walked to the office. Directly she had entered Sylvia slammed the door shut and pushed her into a chair.

'Try and behave a bit normal Babs. Everyone is disgusted at your behaviour. Hans and Paddy are trying to wind Fred up and you are making things worse. They are playing games with you also. If you are not careful you will be fired.'

'Bah! Fired?' As she spoke her voice was slurred and she had difficulty focussing her eyes on Sylvia. 'That's not possible, Hans is the boss. Everybody knows that.' She pushed Sylvia's helping hand away as she struggled to her feet and wobbled back to the bar.

The atmosphere in the salon had deteriorated again. The continuous battle between the partners had created a tension and chill in the air. The girls were getting restless and the number of new clients arriving was steadily dropping. Even the regular clients sensed the change.

'It used to be more relaxed and entertaining here,' complained one of the older regulars, as he was tying up his shoelaces. 'And, by the way the shower gel is up.'

Sylvia watched him leave wondering if he would ever return. She began to ask herself that same question more often when massaging her

138

other clients. In spite of doing her best with her techniques and her cheerful chatter she felt the place had lost its sparkle.

Once again she began to glance through the advertisements.

A couple of weeks had passed. It was midday and Sylvia had just arrived. She had rushed to the salon after receiving a panic call from Fred. Apparently none of the other girls had turned up. Babs had been fired, at last, because of her disruptive behaviour, Manuela had reported sick, Chantal had decided, without giving any reason, not to turn up and Laura was attending some sort of beauty course and would get to work later if possible. In desperation Fred had called her. It was Friday, normally her day off, and reluctantly she had agreed to help out.

It was a hot sticky day and when she arrived she had quickly changed into a flimsy, low cut, short skirted dress. She admired her reflection in the mirror as she sat at the bar drinking a cool glass of white wine, which Fred had given her before disappearing into his office.

She assumed that she and Fred were the only ones in the building and began to touch-up her make-up in case a client turned up. Outside it must have been above thirty degrees and she did not expect many clients, they would either be rushing home early to a barbecue or enjoying a few hours at the beach with their families.

She felt strange being alone in the building, with only the monotonous sound of Fred's voice vibrating softly through the office wall.

Suddenly she heard a noise. It was like a door being opened, and then soft footsteps. Somebody was upstairs. She was about to call Fred when she saw a man appear briefly at the top of the stairs. From a distance he appeared to be a light skinned Indonesian, with a lean build and medium height. He was casually dressed in blue jeans and a brown leather jacket. She saw his eyes looking intently round the rooms below. He must have seen her but gave no indication. After a few seconds he disappeared and she heard another door being opened. Sylvia felt uncertain what to do. The man was obviously not a client; he showed no interest in her.

'Hello Sylvia. I'm glad you were able to make it.'

Sylvia turned her head to see Anita walking in mopping her brow with a handkerchief.

'It's so hot outside,' Anita continued. 'I must sit down and have a cold drink.'

'There is a strange man upstairs,' interrupted Sylvia. 'I've never seen him before. He seems to be inspecting all the rooms.'

'That's right,' answered Anita. 'It must be Sascha. He's a business acquaintance of Fred's, from The Hague. We invited him here. He might be interested in taking over the business.'

'Are you planning to give it up?' Sylvia suddenly looked concerned.

'Oh! Don't worry, not really.' Anita paused, leaned closer and lowered her voice. 'Well I know I can trust you not to tell anyone else. It's just that we are trying to find someone to take over from Hans. This man Sacha has been involved in this sort of business for years and is quite rich.'

She stopped talking as the man began walking down the stairs. Sylvia estimated him to be in his mid forties. He was smoking a cigarette and a strange aroma had wafted down ahead of him, something like camphor or nutmeg.

'Clove cigarettes,' whispered Anita in her ear.

'Sascha, darling, I'm so glad that you were able to make it.' She moved towards him and gave him a kiss on the cheek.

He sat on a stool at the bar, while Anita went behind and found a bottle of Barcardi, reserved for special guests.

'Is your husband still on the phone,' he asked sounding slightly annoyed. He took a swig at his Bacardi cola and looked around. 'He told me that this was a busy salon. Where are all the girls?'

'It's unusually hot today,' said Sylvia, trying to justify the situation.

Sascha raised his eyebrows. 'At my places we are never affected by the weather. Rain, wind or snow, the girls are always on time and the clients keep arriving. That's what I am missing here.'

He turned and looked her up and down. She felt his eyes appraising her as they scanned her face, her breasts and her legs.

'Very nice,' he said, pursing his lips. 'But one masseuse is not enough for a place like this. A few more like you and it would be a gold mine.'

'We do have more girls,' Anita interrupted quickly. 'But unfortunately, today we are having a few problems. Next week we are starting a new advertising campaign.'

'That really shouldn't be necessary.' Sascha spoke like a man talking from experience. 'If you are running a successful business the girls will come to you. At my place I can always choose from several girls waiting for the opportunity to join us. My girls are so satisfied with their work, they always have friends or contacts who would like to try it out. Most evenings it's like a party, for the girls it's more fun than work.'

141

'Except at the end of the evening when half of their income and their costs are deducted.' Anita couldn't resist bringing him back to reality.

He nodded, smiled and eased into a more relaxed posture. 'That's the objective, isn't it? The girls get more than they would earn anywhere else and we get our share of the income. Everybody's happy. That's how it should be here.'

As he spoke to Anita, Sylvia noticed his eyes flicking surreptitiously in her direction. She instinctively sat up straighter and moved one leg elegantly over the other.

'Sitting here waiting for Fred is not a problem with such attractive company.' He said, turning towards her. 'We haven't been introduced yet. What is your name? Would you like a drink?' He moved to a stool next to her.

'Sylvia,' she answered, putting on her well practiced seductive look. 'I'd love a glass of wine.'

From close up she observed that his face was weather beaten, probably from too many hours in the sun and that he had a small scar below his left cheek. He had a sort of rugged attractiveness about him.

Anita discretely disappeared, happy that his attentions were temporarily focussed on Sylvia.

'So, you might be our new boss?' She asked, putting on a naïve expression..

'It's just a possibility. But there are many things to be checked out first. This is not a top class business. It could be improved but it is restricted by its licence and must remain a massage salon. I have two clubs in The Hague and one in Amsterdam. They are well known internationally. I have some high class ladies working for me who are used to wining and dining rich business men and know how to ensure they keep coming back. They can earn thousands a week and some even finish up marrying their clients. I can't see that happening here.'

He paused to light another cigarette before continuing. 'Do you girls have sex with your clients?'

She pretended to be shocked at his blunt way of speaking. He obviously thought she was still inexperienced. He would have been surprised if he knew about her recent escapade.

'Of course not, it's against the rules. This is a massage salon, massage is what they pay for and massage is what they get.'

'If you worked for me you would have to forget all your inhibitions and do what is necessary to satisfy your clients. You would have to make good use of your most valuable asset.'

He laughed, put his hand on her shoulder and stared into her eyes. She felt a persuasive, almost hypnotic, power. For a second she visualised them in a passionate embrace. Maybe he was as good as the American.

'The first time is can be a shock. The second time is a matter of getting used to the idea and from then on it's just for the money. If at the end of the day you get six or seven hundred in your hand, you think ---*that was easy --- *and you look forward to doing even better the next day.'

'You think everybody is just after money, without any principles,' she answered defensively. 'Some of us have other priorities.'

'Principles and priorities won't get you very far in life.' He picked up his glass to finish his drink.

Sylvia looked indignantly at the man who was obviously enjoying himself winding her up.

After a few seconds silence he couldn't resist pushing her further. 'In a place like this you are halfway there. You must get tempted sometimes. If you want to develop your talents you should get some practice with someone with plenty of experience. Why don't you let me help you?'

Sylvia was not sure if he was serious or just teasing. 'Are you joking? I don't even know you.'

He brushed his hand over her hair and played with a curl between his fingers. She felt a tingle of excitement. He radiated self confidence and an erotic charisma which she found difficult to resist.

'I don't know what you mean,' she pretended.

'Let me help you to discover yourself,' His voice was soft and persuasive. 'You are an attractive young lady, you don't realise what potential you have. Let me be your mentor. I can show you pleasure you never even dreamed of. I shall put you on a pedestal and treat you like a princess.'

He sensed her reluctance. 'I'm not like these guys you meet in a disco who expect a quickie after buying you a few drinks. Here's my card. Just give me call and at first I will take you to lunch at a five star hotel. No strings, no commitment, just a friendly meeting for a few hours. You will be well rewarded. For the rest I'm prepared to wait. To wait until you get the desire. Until you feel desperate for some real action. You can choose the time and place. Remember, just a quick phone call and I will give you the time of your life, an experience you will never forget.'

'I'm not sure. Maybe you are going too fast.' She looked at his card, gave him an encouraging smile and put it in her handbag.

They both turned as they heard the office door open and Anita appeared waving a fan under her face, followed by an angry looking Fred.

'Think about my offer,' said Sascha quickly. 'Think carefully and give me a call.'

'I'd better leave you all to your wheeling and dealing.' Sylvia was glad of the chance to escape from such a womanizer. He was an ego tripper and not in the least subtle. On the other hand he was amusing and sexually attractive. For the time being she would keep her options open.

She looked back at them briefly. They were already in serious discussion. It seemed coincidental that no clients were turning up; as if they had somehow sensed that they were not welcome this day.

As she went down to the changing room she tried to visualise the situation if Sascha took over the business. How long would she be able to resist his sexual advances?

Out of boredom she tidied up her locker. Then noticing that the sauna was turned on, she threw off her clothes, grabbed a bath towel and stretched out on the lowest level.

But it was a very warm day and a sauna was the wrong choice. After ten minutes the sweat was running in rivulets down her body. She threw the towel over her shoulders and walked naked towards the shower. Suddenly the door of the men's toilet opened and Sascha appeared in font of her. The towel was stuck to her shoulders as she tried to cover herself.

His mouth fell open and his eyes almost popped out. Then he took a step closer, pulled the towel free and dropped it on the floor.

She made no attempt to move and felt an irresistible thrill of excitement as his hands moved onto her breasts. She felt the power of her body, the power to make men desperate. His hands moved down along the curve of her waist, then pulling her closer his arms encircled her and he fondled her bottom. She could feel something large and stiff between his legs. Her legs relaxed instinctively, opening slightly as his hand moved between them. Her body was glowing with energy, down to her toes, as his fingers played expertly with her pussy. Suddenly, she stepped backwards, picked up the towel and threw it around her.

They both knew it was not the time or place to go any further. Not a word had been spoken; it had been purely sexual arousal.

He went back up to the bar while she dressed and checked her make-up. She could hear the loud and agitated voices of Fred and Anita. She waited a few minutes until they had calmed down before going back up to the bar.

She noticed that Sascha had disappeared, and Fred had collapsed, mentally exhausted, on one of the settees, with a glass of beer, as she sat on a stool close to Anita.

'He's making a call to his partner in Aruba,' said Anita with a frustrated look on her face.

'Why does he have to do that? Sylvia looked surprised. 'He is the boss isn't he?

Anita sighed. 'For a take-over a new limited company has to be set up. Apparently that is only possible if that guy in Aruba agrees. We were hoping everything would go smoothly, but there seems to be complications.' Then still looking a little despondent she shrugged her shoulders and grabbed a bottle of wine. 'I need a drink. Will you join me?'

Eventually the erratic drone, in what sounded like a foreign language, stopped, and Sascha came back to the bar and sat on the stool next to Sylvia.

'I've explained all the options and possibilities and used all my powers of persuasion. Now we just have to wait until tomorrow. Then he will call me back. Let's hope it worked.' He gesticulated with his hands, to emphasise his message to Anita.

'Now I need a strong drink. How about you Sylvia?'

Sylvia leaned closer to him. 'Well yes, I'd like something stronger than this wine. How about a Johnny Walker?'

Anita poured them both a large whisky and left the bar to go and console Fred.

Sascha and Sylvia clinked glasses and she took a large swig of the potent yellow liquid. He still had a stern look on his face and she knew she had to make him relax. She felt in a mischievous mood and teasingly moved her leg over his and put her hand on his knee. He responded immediately and looked challengingly into her eyes as he moved her hand slowly upwards, until she could feel how large and stiff he was. She was now making him desperate as she moved her fingers up and down.

He couldn't resist the invitation and moved his hand up under her pants. She eased herself to the edge of the seat and opened her legs to make it easy. She was amazed how juicy she was and how randy she felt. If they had been alone she would have been on her back already.

145

'Give me a chance,' he whispered in her ears. 'I will take you to the Hilton and give you champagne and lobster.' All you have to do is say when. And then! ......' He brushed his lips over her cheek.

'Then .....? She repeated the word.

'Then I will strip you naked, play with your delicious body until you are begging me to fuck you and then fuck you until you are begging me to stop.'

She pretended to be shocked, pushed his hand away and sat up straight.

He laughed, put his arm around her and pulled her closer.

'Never play games with a man like me,' he teased. 'I can keep going for hours. I have the condition of a race horse. Once I get inside you, you will be in paradise.'

He gave her kiss on her mouth, got up and went to say goodbye to Fred and Anita.

As he went out the door he turned and put his hand up to his ear, as a reminder that she should call.

Sylvia had quickly learned, during weekends, to switch off her thoughts about the salon, leave behind any excitements or problems, and revert to her normal, everyday life at home, together with her family and friends. By the time she started work the following Monday Sascha was no longer dominant in her thoughts. Their teasing talk and seductive games had been fun, but the impact had quickly faded. He was already slotted into her memory as just another escapade. She took out his card and looked at it with amusement. *Another souvenir,* she thought, dropping it back into her bag.

That day, and for the rest of the week, the atmosphere in the salon could be cut with a knife. Fred and Anita started off looking optimistic, waiting for the good news from Sascha. Each day they contacted him on the phone and each time he tried to convince them that it was a matter of time and that negotiations were continuing. Each day they became more depressed. Fred moped around like a bear with sore head. Anita's cheerful laugh had vanished and she was quickly irritated.

The other girls; Laura, Chantal and Manuela, suspected that something serious was going on and that they were being kept in the dark.

Sylvia did her best to help out and keep the business running as normal. She answered the phone, gave the clients coffee and explained the menu. She massaged her clients as normal, but was also unsettled by the tension and uncertainty.

By the end of the week Fred and Anita had to face reality. Sascha had gone back to Aruba and was almost impossible to reach by phone.

'It must be that guy in Aruba that's screwing things up,' complained Anita, with an angry look on her face, when Sylvia asked her how things were going. 'Apparently his name must go on the contract and he is obviously not interested.'

'Why can't Sascha sign the contract?' Sylvia asked.

Anita looked at her with wide open eyes, for a moment hesitating to explain.

'Sascha doesn't exist.' She said abruptly. 'At least, not officially in Holland. If they knew he was here, the tax authorities would have him picked up immediately, for tax evasion.'

'It was a long shot anyway,' she continued, shaking her head. 'Even if Sascha and his partner had been interested, there was no guarantee that Hans would be prepared to sell. Even if he was the price would probably have been too high. We just have to forget the whole idea and concentrate on surviving by our own means.'

Sylvia reacted sympathetically, but was secretly relieved that she didn't have to see Sascha any more.

Anita had built her hopes up far too high and was now so disappointed that she stayed away from the salon for several days. She spent most of her time at home, on the pretext that she had a migraine. Fred also spent half his time at home trying to comfort her. Sylvia felt obliged to help out and continued to deal with the telephone and the customers. She put Fred's home number in her mobile and kept it by the coffee machine, in case of emergency.

The other girls felt neglected and were not cooperating. Chantal, who had always struggled to earn enough to survive on, decided to leave and return her old club. Babs and Manuela, hoping to promote their show business careers, had both succeeded in being taken on as go-go dancers in a popular bar in Amsterdam. Laura continued, but was more interested in making her own contacts and arriving at her own convenience.

More masseuses were desperately needed, and Fred began a new advertising campaign. Even Hans van der Terp began to get involved. Since the disappearance of Sascha, the communication between them had resumed on a more business like basis.

For the next few days Sylvia was non-stop busy. Being the only girl available, she was massaging six or seven clients a day and at the same time trying to keep the place tidy, doing the washing up, vacuuming the carpets and answering the phone when Fred was absent.

Eventually help arrived. A voluptuous black lady walked in. She had bouncy black curly hair, held in place with a brightly coloured Bandana. She wore a long red skirt and a glistening red blouse. She was almost as wide as she was tall and looked like she had just stepped out of a Rio carnival. She had small shiny brown eyes and an enormous row of white teeth.

'Hello,' she spoke in a loud, cheerful, deep voice. 'Is this Body Line?'

'Yes,' answered Sylvia. 'Are you looking for someone?'

'Hans van der Terp suggested that I come here. He's already spoken to your boss, Fred, about it. He told me that you don't have enough girls. So! I thought to myself; *maybe this is a chance for me*. I don't know what sort of place this is, but not enough ladies, means not too much competition. Her eyes swept around the salon, obviously calculating it's potential.

'I'd love a cup of coffee,' she said. 'I've been walking for hours trying to find this place.'

'Are you a masseuse?' Sylvia asked

'Not precisely, I am used to going further. Then I can earn more. I have a couple of little mouths at home who need feeding. There doesn't seem to be much action here at the moment,' she continued, frowning. 'Where are all the customers?'

'Well, it's a bit quiet at the moment, mainly because some of our best girls have just left. It will soon pick up again. It usually does.' Sylvia picked up the program book. 'You had better read this. We do have certain rules here and have to conform to our licence agreement. This is a massage only salon.'

The black lady shrugged her shoulders. 'Rules are made to be broken. What goes on in the rooms is difficult to control.' She smiled knowingly. 'That's between you and your client isn't it?'

She placed her well endowed derrière on a stool and stuck out her hand. 'I'm Zaida and you must be Sylvia. Hans told me that you had red hair.'

'That's right.' Sylvia shook the rather sweaty hand, which she found surprisingly soft. She poured them both a coffee. *Good heavens* she thought. *Do I have to work with such a character?* She tried to imagine the reactions of the regular clients.

'I'm only intending to stay here for a short period, until you have found enough new girls,' said Zaida, trying to reassure her.

'In a months time I'm going to work in Utrecht.'

'In another massage salon?'

'Certainly not,' Zaida laughed at her naïve question. 'I can see that you haven't been in this business very long. Haven't you heard about the Eros boat they are planning to set up in an old dockyard. The idea is to get the us ladies off the streets and into a controlled location. Anyway I managed to get my name on the list for a room there.'

'Won't you have to stand behind a window?'

'Yes, of course, but that's the fastest way to make money, and that's the main objective, isn't it?' She spoke as though it was as normal as any other job. 'If I can stay here for a while, it will be like a vacation. A paid vacation I hope.'

While they drank their coffee Sylvia hoped that it would be a quiet afternoon and that Zaida would be discouraged and leave. Unfortunately she seemed to have all the time in the world and was quite happy to sit and chat and drink coffee. Eventually she had a look round the salon and changed her clothes. She returned to the bar wearing tight fitting, shiny leather pants and a matching top with low cleavage, exposing her large bosom. She was slightly shorter than Sylvia and, although heavily built, moved with surprising agility. Her flesh was firm and her breasts stuck out like melons.

A man entered and sat at the bar, he looked sideways at Zaida, then leaned over the bar and whispered to Sylvia. 'Are there any other girls here?'

'Just me and her, some girls are on holiday at the moment.'

He looked round nervously as Zaida stood up and began to move closer, like a panther about to pounce.

'I... I... I think I'll come back another time.' he stammered, as he stood up and rushed to the door.

'A scared rabbit,' complained Zaida. 'I know that type. He needs to be taken under control and shown how to enjoy himself.'

Sylvia laughed mockingly. 'That's not the way we work here. We try to be more subtle.'

Zaida ignored her remark. 'This place needs cleaning up,' she said, running her finger tips lightly over the bar surface. Then she held a wine glass up under one of the bar lights, exposing a few finger prints. Next she went to the coffee table, sat down and blew some dust off the surface. Then she put her hand under the glass and, with her finger, wrote her name in the clouded surface.

She looked at Sylvia 'Sometimes, for a change, I work for a cleaning company, so I'm quite an expert. It's quiet here at the moment so why don't you find me a bucket and some cleaning material, then we can get into action.'

As she went downstairs Sylvia wondered whether she should call Hans and tell him he had sent the wrong type of person. But ten minutes later, when she saw Zaire working enthusiastically cleaning and polishing the bar, rinsing the glasses and spraying the coffee table she changed her mind. She realised she could do with the help. The air in the salon now had a healthy smell of chlorine and lemon. She joined in, cleaning the bar stools and rearranging the bottles suspended above the bar, at the same time listening to Zaida's life story.

'Finished,' exclaimed Zaida, giving a final polish to the large mirror behind the bar. 'Now we are ready for all those desperate customers. But there's just one more thing necessary,'

Sylvia watched in amazement as Zaida searched under the bar until she found a saltcellar. She walked round the bar to the front door, at the same time opening the saltcellar and pouring some salt in her hand. She opened the door and with her back to the street threw the salt over her left shoulder on to the pavement.

'This will bring us good luck,' she said, brushing her hands together. 'All we have to do now is sit and wait.'

Sylvia poured them both a glass of wine. She watched with amusement as Zaida adjusted her cleavage and positioned herself in a strategic position facing the door, like a spider, ready to lure the first man who entered into her web.

And, to their surprise, before they had finished their wine the first victim walked in; a rather timid, middle aged man with a sad look on his face.

Zaida immediately welcomed him with a cheerful smile. 'Hello sir, why don't you take a seat? It's so warm outside, how about a nice cold beer?'

He hesitated for a few seconds, then smiled and sat on the stool next to her. Sylvia poured him a beer and then moved away, pretending to be busy tidying the coffee cups.

'It's the first time I've been to one of these places,' he said to Zaida nervously. 'Before my divorce I would never have even thought about it. But that was almost a year ago.' He began to look sad again and took a quick swig at his beer.

'I know how you feel. I've been through the same process myself,' said Zaida sympathetically, putting her hand on his arm. 'Why don't you bring your beer with you? We can go upstairs and you can tell me the whole story.'

Sylvia suddenly felt a surge of admiration for Zaida, as she watched them disappearing up the stairs. She seemed to have a talent for putting people at their ease. Although she still thought she was the wrong type for the salon, she realised it was for a couple of weeks only and her stay coincided with a shortage of girls.

She put on some romantic orchestral music to provide a soothing background for them in the massage room. At the bar it was quiet again and out of boredom she decided to do something useful. She began to make an inventory of the snacks and drinks in stock.

After an hour they had still not returned. The sad mouse must have been aroused under the soft hands of Zaida. He had fallen under her spell. He had been transported to a world of relaxation and erotic pleasure. Sylvia's imagination began to carry her away, as usual.

As she crouched down to check the contents of the fridge she was suddenly horrified to notice a large ladder in her stocking. She jumped up and rushed down to her locker. It had become second nature for her to always look neat and sexy, ready for the next client to walk in. This was unacceptable.

She sat on a chair, looking at her reflection in the mirror, as she gently pulled on a new pair of black stockings. She was intrigued by the reflection looking out at her. Was that attractive, sophisticated and sensual young lady really her? Was that the same naïve young girl who had so daringly entered Body Line five months ago? It gave her a thrill to see the slender body, the curvaceous lines, the long, curly, red hair and the long sexy legs.

To pass the time she began to try on different combinations of skirts and tops she had accumulated in her locker. She put on a silver grey mini skirt to contrast with the black stockings, and black shiny shoes with long silver stilettos heels. When she moved her legs a tantalising glimpse of white thigh flashed below her skirt. Then she put on a close fitting silver top with a low cleavage revealing her well formed breasts. As a final touch she put on a wide, shiny, black belt with a bright chrome buckle.

She moved closely to the mirror and began scrutinising and adjusting her make-up; touching up her lipstick, checking her eyeliner and running her fingers through her hair.

'Hello! Is anybody there?'

A man's loud voice jolted her back to reality.

'Won't be a minute,' she shouted, throwing her make-up into her bag and rushing up stairs.

A tall good looking young man with dark blond hair was sitting at the bar. She estimated him to be in his mid thirties. He was elegantly dressed, in a pin striped grey suit, white shirt and striped blue and grey tie. He raised his eyebrows and stared in surprise as she walked towards him, like a model on the catwalk. His eyes stared at her legs, moved up to her breasts and then to her face.

He cleared his throat to regain his composure.

'I was just about to leave.' He spoke in a cultured accent with a slight accent. 'But now I have certainly changed my mind.' he looked at her with sparkling blue eyes and a broad smile. 'What a surprise to find such a charming lady in a place like this. Are you here alone?

Sylvia spread her hands as a sign of apology. 'If you are interested in a massage I'm afraid I am your only choice.' She moved behind the bar, introduced herself and handed him the little brown book. 'Shall I make you a coffee while you choose a program?'

As she spoke they heard a door opening upstairs and they both looked up in amazement, to see Zaida, clad in a bath towel, appearing at the top of the stairs, followed by her client, looking confused and exhausted, wearing a half open bath robe.

'My god,' mumbled Sylvia's visitor, quickly turning his eyes back to the bar.

Zaida led her client down the stairs, with a self satisfied smile. 'Follow me. We can shower and change downstairs,' she said in a loud and bossy voice.

When they had disappeared, the visitor gave her a cynical smile and began to look through the programs.

'By the way, my name is Erik,' he said dropping the brown book back on the counter and looking into her eyes. 'I'm not in a hurry; shall we take an hour body to body? You're the expert. I'll leave the details to you. But first let's have a drink together. Do you have some of white wine, preferably chilled?

Sylvia searched through the cooler and managed to find a bottle of Chardonnay.

'Perfect,' he said, as they touched glasses.

She quickly observed his stylish hair cut, his manicured hands, his well cut suit and his self assured manner. He was unusually good looking and when he looked at her with his penetrating blue eyes she felt a pleasant tingling sensation flowing through her body.

He opened a packet of cigarettes, carefully shaking one loose and offering it to her.

'Do you smoke? Would you like one?'

'Occasionally,' she pretended, trying to hold the cigarette as elegantly as possible between her fingers.

She glimpsed the sparkle of a small diamond set in a gold ring on his right hand as he flicked on his lighter. She puffed on the cigarette without inhaling.

'Where are you from?' she asked, still curious about his accent.

'Not far away. I'm one of your neighbours; I'm from Antwerp.'

'So, are you here on business, or just looking for fun?'

'Both I suppose. I had a meeting this morning with one of my clients who lives in Rotterdam, not far from here. He's having divorce problems with his Belgium wife. I was passing this place on the way back to my car and got curious.'

'You must be a lawyer then?' she asked, moving her cigarette away from her face and giving a little cough.

'What do you think of this place?'

'It's quite cosy and relaxing, and fortunately not too busy. I don't like crowded bars. It's nice to be able to relax with such an attractive lady.' As he spoke he gently took hold of her wrist, and removed the cigarette from her fingers.

'I don't think you were enjoying that,' he said, stumping it out in the ashtray. 'Why don't you come and sit next to me and tell me about yourself?'

She walked round the bar and sat on the stool next too him. They took their time finishing the bottle of wine, while she told him the highlights of her life. He listened sympathetically, asking the right questions and laughing at her humoristic remarks. As they continued their polite conversation she sensed the erotic tension building up between them. She made subtle teasing movements with her legs, adjusted her cleavage when it revealed too much and fondled the stem of her glass suggestively, and all the time looking at him with innocent but seductive eyes.

Eventually he could restrain himself no longer. He emptied his glass, put his hand round her shoulder and pulled her close.

'I think it's time to see these in action,' he whispered in her ear. He took one of her hands in his and played sensually with her long slender fingers.

She was suddenly felt a warm surge in her cheeks. She was horrified. She was blushing. *'That's never happened before,'* she thought. *'What's this man doing to me?'* She jumped up to hide her embarrassment.

'O.K., follow me,' she said, taking his hand.

As they made their way down to the changing room they were both relieved when Zaida and her mouse passed them on their way up to the bar.

She organised his locker, provided him with a bath towel, bath robe and slippers, and while he was showering, rushed up to prepare her favourite massage room. This time everything must be perfect. On the way down she went behind the bar to put on a suitable CD.

Zaida had just shown her client out and was laughing cheerfully. 'The salt trick seemed to have worked. One client each, already and it's still early. Maybe we should do this everyday.'

She closed the door of the massage room, and as she turned she could not believe her eyes. She was looking at a perfect athlete, tall and slender, with rippling muscles glowing in the dim light of the flickering candles. Her heart jumped a beat as he stepped towards her, put his arms round her and kissed her gently. Then he sat on the bed and watched her intently as she teased him with an erotic striptease. As she approached the bed he turned, laid face downwards and closed his eyes.

'Take your time,' he murmured. 'I want this dream to last forever.'

She moved carefully above him, sprinkled some oil over his back and began to massage him, tenderly and rhythmically. Up and down, round, and round, hard and soft. First she massaged his back and waist, then his arms and shoulders and then his legs and thighs. She felt the firm flesh relaxing under her fingers. She worked with pleasure doing her best to satisfy her client.

'Time to turn over,' she said, after ten minutes.

As she moved into position above him and leaned forward he couldn't resist gently fondling her breasts. She pushed his arms firmly down to the bed.

'Take your time. Make it last.' She reminded him. 'Why don't you shut your eyes, and enjoy your dreams?'

She felt her own sexual desires increasing; she fantasised about what was eventually going to happen, and had to force herself to concentrate on her massage treatment. She went through her usual routine for the next ten minutes, slowly building up the tension, purposely avoiding contact with his more intimate parts. But she could not resist stopping sometimes and admiring his penis, sticking up, long and stiff, begging for attention. It seemed to have an independent existence, a mind of its own.

He opened his eyes and grinned. 'You are a fantastic masseuse, but I can't stand it any longer.' He took her hands and guided them downwards. 'This thing will explode if it doesn't get some treatment.'

He groaned as she stroked it gently with her finger tips. Then she began playing with it, like a professional, using all the tricks she had learned. She knew precisely when he was getting too close to a climax and how to calm him down. Then she would begin again. It was a game she had played many times before, but this time she was extra careful not to finish him off. That must be saved for her own pleasure later.

She leaned forward, bending her arms to carry most of her weight and lowering her body on to his and giving him a sensual body to body massage, sliding up and down, round and round, with her breasts and tummy.

'*Incroyable*,' he moaned, putting his arms around her and pressing her closer. She felt his stiff penis trapped between her thighs.

'Mon amour,' he continued, whispering in her ear. 'Je me suis très content tu te connaître. Je suis très heureux.' *(My darling, I am so happy to have met you. You make me very happy).*

She stopped moving, listening in amazement to his sexy voice.

'How romantic,' she answered. 'Are you always so flattering to ladies?'

'Not usually. But you are so irresistible, and I am having such a wonderful time.'

'Well, in that case you deserve some special treatment. Close your eyes again.' She moved her body downwards, slowly lowered her head and took the top of his penis in her mouth. She felt his body jerk in ecstasy as she moved her head up and down, each time pushing it in, deeper. She continued for several minutes, using her fingers, her mouth and her tongue, and varying her movements and speed. His body jerked in spasms of ecstasy, until he could stand it no longer,

'Stop,' he cried, moving her head away. 'I'm almost losing control.'

He pulled her down on the bed next to him and they lay still for a while, relaxing and cuddling each other.

'Now it's your turn,' he said, pushing her on her back and moving on top of her. He picked up the bottle of oil and tipped some into his hands.

She felt a thrill of excitement as his hands moved over her body, He tenderly massaged her arms and shoulders, her chest and breasts and played with her nipples. Then he moved lower, around her waist, along her hips, down her legs to her feet, and then back, slowly and teasingly up the inside of her legs. She felt an irresistible desire surging through her body, and raised her knees and eased her legs apart invitingly. She shut her eyes as his head moved between them and she felt the warmth of his tongue caressing her intimately. She was transported into wild erotic fantasies.

He leaned back, moved his body closer and began to caress her pussy with the tip of his penis. He pressed it against her and paused. 'Do you want me to stop?

'Oh no.' she moaned. Reaching down with her hand and guiding it into her. 'Don't stop, just fuck me, fuck me hard.'

He lifted her legs high and wide and, with a few gentle pushes, was deep inside. He paused for a few seconds, enjoying the moment, the kick of achieving the first penetration into a beautiful woman. Then the real action began. For the next half hour, their bodies took control; they were locked in a non-stop embrace of passion, giving and receiving pleasure, moving in unison. Occasionally he would stop, look into her eyes, kiss her on the mouth and exclaim something that was beyond her schoolgirl French.

When she realised he was getting too excited and nearing a climax, she gently pushed him out, rolled on to her side and sat up.

'What are you doing?' he asked, looking confused. 'I haven't finished yet.'

'I know,' she said, fondling his penis which was still hard as a rock. 'But you were getting too excited. I'm sure you like variation. Why don't you finish me off from behind?'

His eyes lit up with enthusiasm. 'Great idea, I haven't done that for years.'

She knelt on the bed, with her knees slightly apart and lowered her head and shoulders. This was her favourite fantasy position, to be completely at the mercy of a man she could not see but only feel. He placed his hands on her hips and gently entered into her. He started slowly and began to sing little love songs. Then he began to move faster and she felt surges of uncontrollable erotic energy flowing through her body. She was losing control, and began breathing heavily and making moaning noises. He sensed that she was getting close and her reaction made him so excited that he moved faster and harder until they both exploded in violent simultaneous orgasms.

They collapsed on the bed next to each other and lay still for several minutes, looking at their reflections in the mirror above.

She ran her fingers tips lightly over his body and was surprised to feel him becoming erect again.

'I think it's waking up,' she said, taking it in her hand and waving it backwards and forwards. 'How about another quick treat before you leave?'

He did not resist as she sat up, leaned forward and took it in her mouth, and at the same time put her hand round it, moving up and down, faster and faster. It quickly became completely hard and she continued relentlessly with her hand movements, determined to finish him off a second time. Within a few minutes his body began jerking uncontrollably. She sucked hard and felt his penis pulsating, as the warm liquid spurted into her mouth. He lay still, almost paralysed, as she reached for the tissues.

'I've never had such a fantastic experience,' he said, when he had recovered, sitting up and reaching for his bathrobe. 'But now, unfortunately its time for me to leave, just time for a shower and a farewell drink.'

She quickly tidied up the massage room and followed him down to the changing room. As she walked down the stairs she was amazed to see Zaida's reclining on the settee like the Queen of Sheba. She was obviously still enjoying her first success. She had put on some soft romantic music, and had placed some candles on the bar and coffee table, and had fixed herself a Bacardi and coke. She waved to Sylvia, with an expression that said; *'We make a good team, don't we? We have both made a man happy.'*

When she reached the changing room he was already busy in the shower, singing loudly. She threw off her bath towel and was about to step into the adjacent shower when his door opened and he reached out and pulled her in with him. 'Share a shower and save the environment,' he said with a big grin.

Sylvia poured out two coffees and sat next to him at the bar. He was still in an amorous mood and put his arm round her waist. 'I want to take you with me, to my villa in Antwerp,' he said enthusiastically. 'Who can stop me? I shall put you in my car and whisk you away. Nobody will miss you here?'

'I will!' They were startled by Fred's voice. He had entered by the rear door and they had not heard him approach. He was smartly dressed in a dark suit and his hair neatly brushed back. Apparently he had been to a family gathering. Since the Sascha fiasco he took every opportunity to extend his family contacts.

He laughed friendly, but with a possessive air, towards her client. 'So! You are busy trying to steal one of my best girls. She belongs here.' He turned to Sylvia. 'You are satisfied with your work here, aren't you?'

She nodded, rather hesitantly.

Fred nodded back approvingly, then turned up the music volume and

159

took a bottle of champagne out of the cooler. 'Why don't we all have a nice cool drink and calm down?'

Sylvia pressed closer to Erik and they began to sway, like young love birds, to the heavy beat of Abba.

Zaida joined Fred behind the bar as he popped the cork and filled some glasses. 'How touching,' she said, raising her glass towards them. 'Love at first site. Can we all come to the wedding?'

Sylvia sensed that they were mocking them and pressed closer to Erik. 'How do you survive here?' He whispered. 'I think we must have a serious conversation soon'

He finished his glass and asked Fred for the bill.

'I'd like to take her out for dinner. Can you miss her for a couple of hours?' He asked, as he counted out the money.

Fred shook his head emphatically. 'Sorry, it's just not possible. We are hopelessly short of girls.'

Sylvia went with him to the door and they stepped outside to say goodbye. He pulled her close and kissed her passionately 'I will be back soon and we can talk further.'

'Call me soon.' She called, as he walked away.

She finished the rest of the day in a daze, trying to ignore the questioning looks of Fred and Zaida.

The next morning, after a restless nights sleep dreaming about his caresses, his singing and his charming and persuasive manners. Sylvia woke feeling somewhat disorientated. It was a feeling that she had never experienced before. It was a mixture of elation and concern.

What is happening to me? She thought as a myriad of questions flashed through her mind. *Am I losing control? Why do I have such a strange yearning feeling? Am I being foolish? Was he really being sincere? What do I know about him? Is he married? Does he have children?*

She had to make an effort to concentrate on her make-up, and had no appetite for breakfast. When she arrived at the salon she did her best to act normal, trying to hide her emotional turmoil. Zaida was too busy cleaning the changing room and showers to ask any inquisitive questions and Fred was busy in his office.

Fortunately, within ten minutes, one of her regulars turned up and she could concentrate on keeping him satisfied. She was relieved that it was a table massage only. In her present state of mind she was not in a hurry to give a body to body. She imagined that somehow it would be a betrayal of her commitment to Erik.

After weeks of advertising for girls, Fred had at last succeeded in finding two new candidates, both young girls without previous experience. The first girl arrived shortly after Sylvia had finished with her first client. She was a small, pleasant, rather plain looking young girl, with a round pale face and short blond hair. Her uninspired clothes were obviously chosen disguise her chubby figure. She had finished her school studies and had moved from her village in Zeeland to stay with an Aunt in Rotterdam, in the hope of finding work.

Fred called Sylvia into the office to introduce her. 'This is Nancy,' he said, putting his hand on her shoulder like a concerned father. 'She's new to this sort of work but would like to try it out for a few days. Would you mind showing her round, explaining her duties and helping her settle in?'

Sylvia nodded. *Another lamb to the slaughter*, she thought, as she shook the girl's hand. *I wonder how long she will last.*

Sylvia did her best to put her at her ease. She showed her the massage rooms and the facilities downstairs. Then they sat at the bar drinking coffee while Sylvia explained the programs and prices.

'It's only massage? asked Nancy, suddenly looking worried. 'I mean, I know its erotic massage. But how far do I have to go?'

'It's always difficult at the beginning,' answered Sylvia, realising she had to put her at her ease. 'Why don't you tell Fred that, for the first few days, you only want to do table massages? Then when you feel you can handle it, you can progress further, step by step, to more intimate massages. Remember the further you go the more you earn. You have to forget your inhibitions and learn how to use your hands and body. In any case real sex is not allowed. You must learn when to say no, if a client gets too aroused, and to keep him under control.'

She frowned at Nancy's clothes. They were not at all suitable. She was wearing a light blue, loosely fitting blouse, a long dark blue skirt and dark blue flat shoes. *With a little make-up, a sexy outfit and some high heels,* she thought, *she could look ten times more attractive.*

'Have you brought some working clothes with you?' she asked, 'something that would appeal more to clients?'

'Well, no. I thought that today I was just coming for an interview. But Fred suggested I stay for a few hours to get the feel of the place. I will bring something more suitable tomorrow.'

Fred was glad to have found someone new, and although she was not a top glamour girl, he knew she would appeal to some clients, especially the ones on his secret list. She was young and inexperienced, and some men got a kick out of being the first to try out a new girl. Sylvia noticed him behind the bar looking through his little black book. He poured himself a beer, lit a cigarette and disappeared into his office.

For the next few hours Nancy was not chosen, and she sat on the settee closely observing everything that was happening, especially watching Sylvia's moves when one of her clients turned up.

Eventually Fred's telephone calls paid off. One of the clients on his list turned up, obviously hoping to be the first customer to try out the new young masseuse. Looks were not his main consideration. Fortunately he was quite a young and sympathetic character, who would give her plenty of encouragement.

Nancy's eyes opened wide. She was relieved to be chosen at last, but also nervous about what was expected from her. As the man took her arm to lead her upstairs, she looked like a frightened rabbit, but she also had a determined look in her eyes.

The next day the second new recruit arrived. Her name was Valerie, also young and inexperienced. She was no beauty, but had a slender and shapely figure, and long shiny brown hair. She was more attractive than Nancy.

Sylvia went through the same introduction routine. She wondered whether she was training her own competition, but was glad of the distraction. She preferred to be kept occupied, whenever she had a quiet period that lasted too long, her thoughts automatically drifted back to her encounter with Erik. *He had promised to contact her soon. Why was he taking so long?*

The two new girls had a lot in common and after a few days were close friends. Sylvia was amused to see how quickly they got over their inhibitions. They began to experiment with their make-up and compete with each other for the sexiest outfits and the highest heels, and also who could get the most clients. Valerie, with her slim figure was usually the winner.

Although Nancy was not occupied most of the time, Sylvia noticed that she took a considerable interest in the salon, and she kept asking her lots of questions.

'Do you find this place interesting?' asked Sylvia.

'Well yes. I'm curious how much it would cost to run a place like this.'

'No idea. Are you interested then?' Sylvia asked, in a mocking voice. 'It's not only the salon that you take over; you are stuck with a long term contract and all the usual running costs.'

'I understand,' she sighed. 'But it's such a pity that it isn't better organised. It could be a gold mine.'

'I agree with you there. But if you want more information you have to ask Fred or Hans van der Terp, they make the policies.'

'In my opinion there is no policy,' said Nancy, emphatically, as though she knew better.

'Well, if you can do better, let us know.' Sylvia was losing interest in the girl's daydreams and was relieved to see her Professor waving to her from the bar.

Zaida had lost interest in the salon. Since the arrival of the young girls she was lucky to get one client a day. The Eros boat was finally ready to open and after several phone calls to her contacts in Amsterdam she had persuaded them to reserve a place for her. But she didn't leave without

163

taking at least one of her victims with her. On her last evening Sylvia noticed her giving a slip of paper to one of her few clients, obviously someone who liked the full treatment.

Fred began to spend more time away from the salon, visiting friends and business acquaintances. He was desperately looking for alternative business opportunities. Together with Anita he investigated the possibility of dealing in massage oils; supplying other salons and health centres. Another possibility was to import batik shirts and blouses from Indonesia. But after expending much time and effort not much materialised. Their main problem was finding the capital to get started.

Sometimes the new girls would get into a frivolous mood and chatter and giggle non-stop. If it lasted too long Sylvia would escape to the sauna or the whirlpool.

One afternoon she was relaxing in the whirlpool reminiscing back to the fun times with Laura, Alexandra, Puck and Babs. Back to the time when she was new and inexperienced, and everything seemed so exciting. Now she was the only one of the old team left, and even at her young age she was the senior girl, the girl with the experience, the girl that knew everything, looked up to by the new girls. It put her in an unavoidable position of responsibility, a position she had not sought and was not happy with. She was getting restless and yearned for some new excitement. *When, oh when was Erik going to contact her?* The bubbles stopped and the program was up. Feeling slightly deflated she stepped out of the bath.

She returned to the bar just as a strange looking character walked in. He was in his early thirties, rather short and podgy, with a pallid complexion. He was dressed to give the impression of a real macho man. Obviously a fan of Elvis Presley, he had thick black hair and long sideboards, kept in place with half a tube of gel. He was wearing a black embroidered shirt, partly open at the front revealing a gold chain. There was a slight bulge over his tight jeans. A bunch of keys was suspended from his black belt and he was carrying what looked like a metal briefcase.

'Can I help you?' asked Sylvia.

'My name is Nanno. I'm a friend of Fred's. He asked me to come and help out in the salon.'

'What sort of help?' Sylvia suddenly felt resentful at his intrusion. 'Fred is not here at the moment. He didn't tell us anything about you.'

'Well! He told me that he was spending a lot of time out of the salon and asked me if I could help keep an eye on things when he's not here. He also told me that there are problems with the sound system and some of the electrical equipment.'

'Do you mean the HiFi?' asked Sylvia, suspicious of his competence. 'Are you experienced in that sort of work?

He frowned as though she was asking an impertinent question. 'These are my tools,' he said, laying his metal case on the bar. 'I'm responsible for the sound installation in one of the most famous discos in Rotterdam. I've been working there for years. Sometimes I also help out as a DJ.'

Sylvia sensed the animosity building up between them. 'O.K. Help yourself.' She said, pointing to the HiFi equipment behind the bar.

He immediately began to fiddle with the HiFi controls, and for the next hour had Nancy and Valerie running up and down to each massage room in turn, to check the results of his adjustments. When he was eventually satisfied he turned his attention to the CD's, piling them up on the counter. He opened his tool box and got out some cleaning material, and for the next couple of hours he carefully scrutinised each CD before cleaning it meticulously.

'How can anyone be so sloppy,' he grunted, rubbing some fingerprints off the last CD and placing it carefully in its matching cover. 'Now, I think I've earned a cold beer.'

'I'll check if there's any left in the cooler downstairs,' volunteered Nancy, 'but I think Fred had the last one.'

A few minutes later she returned with a bottle.

'No wonder this place needs some help,' he grumbled, as he poured out the lukewarm beer. 'Tomorrow I will check out your refrigerators.'

Nanno was here to stay. During the next few days he was non-stop busy with his toolbox, first adjusting the refrigerator settings, then the settings for the shower, the sauna and the central heating. He replaced dud light bulbs and serviced the vacuum cleaner. Fred, who didn't know which way round to hold a screwdriver, was impressed. He was no longer dependent on the local plumber or electrician.

Although he was not an expert, Nanno somehow managed to get things working properly, and he was not expensive. He was satisfied with a few euros per hour and his free drinks. Sometimes, as a special reward, Fred would allow him to take a massage for half price. Not from Sylvia, of course, who was horrified at the idea, but from Nancy or Valerie, who had no objection as long as they got their standard fee.

Nanno's work at the disco was mainly on the weekends and he began to spend most of his weekdays at the salon. He seemed to enjoy the status of supervising the salon and the girls and had quickly added a few more keys to his bulging key ring.

He was a music fanatic and reorganised the CD's, into groups, each with its own index. Fred would look on in awe as, within a few seconds, he could find a Fats Domino or an Elvis Presley.

Sylvia tolerated him and was glad she didn't have to spend so much time behind the bar. She could relax more and concentrate on her clients.

The longer Nanno stayed the more self assured he became. Once he had finished all his maintenance activities and had more time on his hands, and especially when Fred was not around, he would assume the role of the manager. He would try to boss the girls, like a keeper at the zoo, although none of them took him very seriously.

Sylvia realised that, in spite of her cool reactions, he secretly fancied her. After a few drinks he would accidentally press too close to her, when they were passing each other, or she would feel his hand brushing over her bottom. When it was quiet in the salon, he would spread himself out on the settee with a beer and a cigar and, with the excuse that he had had a late night at the disco, and pretend to doze off. But she noticed him sneakily watching her, fantasising, as he looked at her legs and sexy outfit. He liked to give the impression he was a bit of a stud, but in reality he was hopelessly unsuccessful with the ladies. She knew she must keep him at a distance; too much familiarity might give him false hope.

Occasionally, to boost his image, he would take a massage from Nancy, but even she found him unattractive. Afterwards she would complain that he used too much deodorant to cover up his rather unpleasant body odour.

Anita and Sylvia both tolerated him while he was useful. On one occasion they were having a wine together and watching him, with amusement, when he was really asleep on the settee.

'Nobody is supposed to know,' said Anita, in confidence, 'but he still lives at home with his mother. His father disappeared years ago.'

'That could explain why he behaves like an old man,' smiled Sylvia. 'He probably never had a real youth and is full of frustrations.'

Summer and autumn had flown by, and winter was beginning to spread its cold damp hand. New ideas were desperately needed to draw in the customers, to get them off the streets and into the warm embrace of the salon. Being relatively new, Nanno was determined to prove that he could help boost the turnover. He would disappear for hours into Fred's office to discuss his latest harebrained ideas.

Eventually they seemed to have found something.

Fred called the girls together at the bar to explain their latest idea. 'With Nanno's help we are going to organise a 'Special Night' and invite as many customers and new contacts as possible.'

'What will be so special? asked Sylvia, suddenly getting interested.

'Well, to attract the clients we need to offer them something special, something more exciting than usual.' Fred was suddenly full of enthusiasm. 'We will ask Roy, our restaurant owner friend, to provide an Indonesian buffet, and we will provide a wider selection of drinks, including some cocktails. Nanno will be the DJ and will provide the music. He will also try to persuade some young ladies, from his disco to join us. It will be on a Saturday evening and we are hoping that we can rely on all of you to turn up. We need all the girls we can get.'

'Count me in,' said Sylvia, waving he hand. 'It could be fun and maybe we can attract some new clients.'

Valerie and Nancy whispered to each other before answering. They were concerned about giving up their free Saturday evening.

'What would we have to do and what would we get out of it?' asked Nancy.

'Well, we need you girls to keep the men amused, to chat with them and maybe dance with them. You should use your charms to persuade them to take a massage with you…. for your usual rates of course.' Explained Fred. 'You will also get a percentage of any drinks they order.'

'But for a Special Night some of them might be expecting some special treatment,' said Valerie looking dubious.

'Don't worry about that,' said Fred, glancing at Nanno. 'One or two of the ladies Nanno invites will be willing to help out in that area.'

167

Over the next two weeks Fred and Nanno were busy with their preparations. Fred added a short notice in his daily advert in the local press. Even Anita became enthusiastic and turned up more often to help and to work out the menu for the buffet with Roy.

Sylvia and the other girls began to get used to the idea and even began to look forward to the event. Fred contacted Laura who also promised to join in.

Fred had arranged for the party to begin at six o clock, in the hope that some guests would be tempted by the buffet instead of going home for their dinner. Several of the regular clients promised to come and Fred had received many enquires from guys intrigued by his advert.

On the day of the party, Sylvia turned up early to help with the preparations and was thrilled when also Laura arrived early. They had a long chat together, catching up with each others recent experiences. Nanno set up his microphone and some more powerful loudspeakers, then rearranged the furniture to create a small dance area in the corner of the room behind the settees.

First to arrive were three players from the local football team. They had just won their match and were keen to celebrate. Fred gave them a welcome free drink and introduced them to Nancy and Valerie. Over the next couple of hours a steady flow of men arrived and a queue quickly formed at the buffet.

As the number of visitors increased Nanno made a phone call, and half an hour later five quite attractive young ladies arrived. They were his disco girls. It soon turned into a swinging evening, and the dance area had to be increased as Nanno persuaded everyone to get up and dance.

As the girls mingled with the guests, the drinks began to flow, including Fred's cocktails. Anita was back in form, helping Fred to welcome the guests as they arrived. At first Sylvia tried to move around, chatting to as many people as possible, but was soon trapped by two of her favourite regulars, the Project Manager and the IT man. She introduced them to each other and found some space on a settee. Fortunately the two men hit it off well together and took it in turns to buy rounds of drinks and to dance with her. She felt a tingle of excitement receiving attention from two men at the same time. They bought her cocktails and tried to outdo each other telling naughty jokes.

Nanno was in his element. He had another idea to brighten up the evening. He spoke to the disco girls, and two of them agreed to his proposal. Then he stopped the music to make an announcement.

'Gentlemen! It's time for some entertainment. Who would like to see a striptease show?' he asked through his microphone.

There was a roar of approval from the men.

'Then this is your lucky night guys. These two gorgeous young ladies have agreed to take part in a striptease competition. I'm sure you know how to show your appreciation,' he said, tapping his finger on his wallet. He then put on some sensual music and turned the lights down low. The disco girls had sexy figures and were quite experienced at striptease. They each gave a sensual and erotic performance. The more money that was thrown at them the more of their, already scanty, clothes they took off. When they were down to their strings there were several cries of; 'Get them off.'

The striptease increased the arousal of the men and the number of couples disappearing to the showers and massage rooms increased. Anita had to start a waiting list for access to the massage rooms.

Sylvia sensed that her two clients were also getting aroused and did not resist when their hands moved on to her knees. They watched in amusement as Nancy and Valerie flirted with the three footballers on the settee opposite. The two girls were drinking too much, giggling like teenagers and sitting on the men's laps. Eventually all five stood up together and went downstairs to the sauna.

'Three men and two girls in the sauna at the same time,' said the Project Manager. 'I think it's going to get hotter than normal in there. I'm getting rather jealous.'

Sylvia grinned. 'Those girls have quickly lost their inhibitions and learned how to enjoy themselves.'

The Project Manager leaned forward and winked at the IT man. 'Don't you think its time we had some fun? I fancy a nice erotic massage from Sylvia. How about you? Would you like to join us?'

Sylvia felt the IT man's hand moving further up her leg. 'I can't wait much longer either,' he whispered in her ear, 'Can you handle two men at once? I'd love to take part in a threesome.'

Sylvia's heart began to pound. She had often fantasised about a session with two men at the same time. She might never get such a chance again, especially with two men she fancied and felt relaxed with.

'Okay. But only if I can decide how far it goes,' she said, pretending to be nervous.' Why don't you both take a shower and organise a bottle of champagne, while I arrange the best room with Anita.'

The men quickly threw off their bathrobes and sat on the bed with their glasses of champagne while Sylvia went through her own striptease show. She undressed slowly and teasingly, moving closer and closer. When she had removed all her clothes they tried to fondle her, but she put her hands on their shoulders and pushed them both down onto their backs. Their erections were sticking up like two flag poles, desperate for attention, and she couldn't resist moving between them and grabbing them both at the same time. She began stroking and tickling with her fingers, and then gripped them firmly, moving her hands up and down. It gave her an incredibly kick; it was a new and exciting experience to hold two stiff penises at the same time. She had great fun playing all her tricks with her hands. From their reactions she knew that they were hoping for something more. She leant forward and made them groan with pleasure as she took each one in turn in her mouth, moving up and down until they almost climaxed.

After ten minutes she rolled on to her back between them, inviting them to take the initiative. Each of them took it in turn to fondle her pussy while the other knelt down to let her play with his weapon. She felt herself becoming very juicy and realised that this was going to be a very naughty session.

There was no stopping half way, and she did not resist when they took it in turns to move on top of her. She opened her legs in invitation and guided them, in turn, into her pussy. They competed with each other to give their best performance. She lay back and enjoyed every minute. It must have been half an hour before they stopped for a pause, to recover their energy and to share the last of the champagne. Then she turned round on to her knees so that they could attack her from behind. She shut her eyes and tried to guess which one was fucking her, and was soon overwhelmed by an incredible climax.

After they had all showered, she joined them at the bar for a parting drink. When they had paid their bills, they both gave her a goodbye kiss and pressed a generous tip into her hand.

'I think you are getting to be as naughty as me.' Laura was smiling at her, as she eased herself on to the stool next to her. 'I've already had two guys as well, but not both at the same time. You are one up on me so far.'

170

She paused to light a cigarette, and then continued. 'Why don't we have a little competition to see who can get the most men during the rest of the evening?'

'Okay,' agreed Sylvia, still feeling in fruity mood. She had noticed a rather handsome man sitting behind Laura. He was pointing at her, then at himself and then in the direction of the stairs. 'Let's put 50 euros on it,' she said with a smile, as she stood up and walked towards her next victim.

The following Monday morning, sitting in the Metro on her way to the salon, Sylvia closed her eyes and let her thoughts drift back to the events of last Saturday night. Her loyalty to Erik had temporarily faded. She still felt excited about her wild escapades and had no regrets; she had enjoyed being so extremely naughty and even felt proud of her performance.

When she arrived, Fred and Anita were already busy cleaning up the mess of empty bottles and beer cans, coffee cups and glasses, piled up dirty crockery and cutlery, and full ash trays.

'Did you enjoy yourself Saturday?' Fred asked, with a cheerful smile. 'It was quite successful, wasn't it?'

'It was better than I expected and I had a great time,' she answered. 'I can hardly remember the last few hours. I think had a bit too much to drink. But, I do remember you organising a taxi home for me.'

'All you girls did very well, especially you and Laura, you were both very popular. We attracted a lot of new faces and I'm sure some of them will return occasionally.' He paused to light a cigarette. 'What do you think of our idea to make it a regular event, possibly once a month?'

'It's not a bad idea. But, don't you have to be careful? It was a bit wild for a place like this. Aren't you worried that Hans might find out and cause problems? We are supposed to be a massage parlour and Saturday night things went much further than normal.'

Fred's smile disappeared. She had apparently touched a sensitive nerve.

'I'm not worried what he thinks,' he snorted, 'Babs and Chantal would still be here if it wasn't for him. He couldn't keep his hands to himself. He couldn't resist taking advantage of his position. He has chased too many of our best girls away, and their clients with them.' He pressed out his cigarette hard into an ash tray and disappeared in his office.

A few minutes later Nancy and Valerie turned up. They were both looking quite cheerful and immediately sat down together, away from the others, and began chatting and giggling. They were obviously discussing their experiences at the party. Sylvia wondered what they had got up to with the footballers.

Shortly afterwards Nanno strutted in, looking around like he owned the place. He had a self satisfied look on his face. 'Wasn't that a great evening?' he asked, obviously fishing for compliments. 'I think I did a great job.'

As nobody responded he went behind the bar and poured himself a coffee. He looked round smugly. 'Over the weekend I've been thinking how we can make even more improvements here.'

After a pause to drink some of his coffee, he continued. Telling them what they already knew. 'We must all try harder to attract the clients and to keep them coming back.'

He looked at Nancy. 'For example Nancy, you could do much better if you dressed sexier, improved your make-up and maybe slimmed down a little. You should try to follow Sylvia's example.' Then he turned to Valerie. 'You should learn to be more self-assured and cheerful when first talking to clients, even if you don't fancy them. They appreciate someone who shows some enthusiasm.'

The two girls sat frowning at each other, but did not protest. They realised that there was some truth in what he was saying.

Next he turned to Sylvia. 'You shouldn't be in such a hurry to rush to the clients when they arrive. You should give the other girls more chance.'

Sylvia gritted her teeth, trying to constrain herself. She felt she could happily put some arsenic in his coffee. The man was becoming too conceited. But she needn't have worried. During the rest of the day, even though he made a point of introducing Nancy or Valerie to new clients first, while leaving her sitting on the settee, she was still chosen by most clients. It even seemed to work to her advantage. When they looked around and saw her they soon realised that Nanno was trying to promote the less attractive girls.

Eventually the inevitable happened. Hans van der Terp had somehow found out about the wild Saturday evening. He turned up without warning, went straight to Fred's office and flung the door wide open.

'What do you think you doing? He ranted. 'Are you trying to ruin our business by turning it into a cheap bordello?'

'It's your own fault,' answered Fred calmly. 'If you charged a reasonable rent we could continue as a normal massage salon. If not, then we are forced to find other ways to survive.'

'If it happens again I will have you thrown out,' shouted Hans. You are risking us losing our licence.'

The office door was slammed shut as the battle continued.

Nanno and Anita frowned at each other and Valerie looked shocked. But Sylvia couldn't help noticing that Nancy had a rather mischievous grin on her face as though she was enjoying the situation. The idea suddenly flashed through her mind that this could explain how Hans had got to hear about the evening.

The sounds were now muffled by the closed door but the row continued. Sylvia decided to escape to the sauna.

Over the next couple of weeks Hans stayed away and Fred continued his struggle to survive. Gradually Sylvia and the other two girls became friendlier towards each other and began working together as a team. Both Nancy and Valerie were gaining confidence and maturing fast. They were also steadily building up a number of regulars. Sylvia was quite intrigued when she noticed that two of the footballers were amongst their regular clients. They both began to look up to Sylvia, as she was still the top performer, and would ask her advice about their outfits, their make-up and their jewellery.

'Don't spend all your hard earned money.' Sylvia advised them. You should try to save something.'

'That's not difficult for me,' Nancy replied. 'My Aunt lives on her own and is glad of my company. She is quite well off and doesn't charge me anything to stay with her.'

Sylvia began to realise that she had underestimated Nancy. Although from a small country village, she had a sharp natural intelligence and took an interest in a wide rang of topics. Her father was a dealer in second hand cars, and had access to several plots of land owned by their family. They were apparently quite and enterprising family.

Suddenly Nancy did not turn up for a few days.

'She has to attend the funeral of her Grandmother.' explained Anita.

When she eventually returned they all showed their sympathy and offered their condolences. Sylvia noticed that although she was upset she also seemed to be excited about something. Eventually they found out that she had inherited a substantial amount of money.

Fred's attitude to Nancy changed immediately. He sensed a possible source of capital, a temporary investment that could carry him over this difficult period. Whereas previously he had just tolerated her, he now began to turn on the charm.

'Take all the time off you need, during this difficult period,' he said sympathetically. 'Let us know if we can be of any help.'

It was a waste of time. Nancy remained aloof towards him. She knew she now had the upper hand. Soon afterwards Sylvia overheard her talking to Valerie.

'I've spoken to Hans, Everything is being arranged. Wait and see….'

They stopped talking when they noticed Sylvia, as she walked past on the pretence of collecting some towels.

Sylvia went down to the changing room and sat down trying to figure out what the conversation could mean. Her head was spinning. Nancy was obviously planning something with Hans. Should she tell Fred what she had heard? No, she decided to wait until the weekend was over.

When she arrived the following Monday morning, Sylvia was surprised to find the door locked. She pressed her nose against the window but it was dark inside with no sign of life. The salon looked ominously still. She waited a few minutes and was about to walk away, to get a coffee in the café round the corner, when she saw Fred's car arriving.

As he walked towards her she noticed the concerned look on his face, his dishevelled hair and his hunched shoulders. The strain was having its impact. He was no longer the enthusiastic entrepreneur who had encouraged them with so much enthusiasm a few months earlier..

'That bastard, Hans van der Terp.' He mumbled, as he fumbled with his keys to open the door. 'He is becoming a menace. Sticking the knife in just when it is going bad with the business.' He turned Sylvia with a desperate look 'What so you think? Can we survive? Are you expecting a few regulars today?

'Maybe you can make more of an effort to help me,' she snapped back irritably. 'You could improve your advertising for a start, or you could make a few telephone calls to encourage your clients.

"Sylvia!" He was shocked at her brutality. 'Such cynicism doesn't suit you. You don't agree with Hans, do you?'

As they entered the salon there was a pronounced smell of stale tobacco. When Fred switched on the lights they saw empty glasses, a full ashtray and some nuts scattered over the bar.

'This mess wasn't here when we closed up Friday evening,' grunted Fred, as he began to clean up the counter. 'Would you mind checking upstairs and down stairs?'

Sylvia found a sleeping bag in one of the massage rooms and a razor in the changing room downstairs. They guessed that it must have been Nanno, he had a key and was obviously making use of the facilities for his own use.

Sylvia changed into a sexy working outfit and sat on her own by the coffee table while Fred finished cleaning up the bar and fiddled with the CD player. He found some relaxing music which he hoped would put customers at their ease. She still felt resentful and was in no hurry to talk to him. Although she sympathised with him she thought he put all the blame on Hans and forgot his own shortcomings.

Fred looked more and more frustrated as they sat waiting for the first customer. To his annoyance Nancy and Valerie had not turned up. Sylvia was prepared to work harder as the clients would have no choice but to choose her. But for the next hour nobody arrived.

Suddenly they looked at the door in anticipation as someone turned the handle. But their enthusiasm quickly changed to dismay as Hans walked in. He ignored Sylvia and began waving some papers at Fred.

'The take-over contract,' he said bluntly. 'We have arranged for Nancy to take over from you.' He threw the papers on the counter. 'All you have to do is sign, and all your troubles will be over.'

For a few seconds Fred's face froze in astonishment and he was unable to speak. When he had recovered his composure he took a deep breath, grabbed the papers and threw them back at Hans.

'So! That's what you have been up to behind my back. Do you really think such a bimbo as Nancy could run a place like this? You must be out of your mind. Well, you can forget it. I'm signing nothing. You better contact my lawyer. I am the legal occupier of this salon and you had better leave before I call the police and have you thrown out. I don't want to see you here again.'

Hans shrugged his shoulders and picked up the papers. 'Have it your way. For now,' he said, as he made his way to the door. 'Soon you will have to face reality. You don't have a leg to stand on.'

Fred lit a cigarette with shaking hands and looked at Sylvia for sympathy. 'If that idiot thinks he can throw me out he's got another think coming. I have invested all my money in this business and am not giving

177

up without a fight. He drew hard on his cigarette and blew out a cloud of smoke. 'I wondered why that girl had been asking so many questions lately, I might have guessed that that she was up to something.'

He put a hand on her shoulder. 'Looks like we have to fight this battle together, Sylvia. Can I rely on your support?'

Sylvia nodded. 'Of course Fred but you really need to make a few changes.'

He let his hand fall. 'We will do everything to survive. But we must first get that guy off our backs.'

Adverts were placed for new girls, but it usually took two or three weeks to find anyone suitable. Sylvia felt a bit lonely, working on her own, without any other girls to chat to. On the one hand it gave her the chance to get more clients, as she was their only choice. But, on the other hand she found it difficult to refuse clients that she didn't fancy.

The two footballers continued to turn up. Luckily they always came on different days. They were both disappointed that Nancy and Valerie had left, but they were also pleased that they now had a chance to choose Sylvia instead. They were handsome and athletic young men and when they choose her she felt she was facing a challenge. She had to show them how much better she was than those two naïve young girls.

While she was chatting at the bar with the first one to turn up, she quickly found out what the two girls had got up to during the special evening party. Apparently they had got a bit tipsy and had had a wild orgy with all three footballers.

'Since then we are used to getting the full treatment,' he said, putting his hand on her arm and raising his eyebrows suggestively.

Sylvia paused before answering. She realised she was trapped, but at the same time felt a sudden irresistible surge of excitement. *Why not?* she thought to herself: *After all the stress and tension I've been going through lately it's about time I had some fun. Especially with such an attractive and virile young man.*

'Well, I'd like to get to know you first,' she answered, with pretence of modesty. 'Let's start in the whirlpool and see what happens.'

Once she was in such a frivolous mood and her naughty urges began to take over there was no doubt about what would happen. Although he didn't realise it, this young man was now her next victim.

In the whirlpool a lot of erotic fondling took place and by the time they reached the massage room they were both desperate, and immediately sprang into action, like frustrated tigers. There were no preliminaries. She pulled him on top and into her and for the next hour there was a frenzy of lustful and energetic action. She forced him to work hard to satisfy her sexual demands.

After showering playfully together, they sat at the bar and shared a bottle of wine.

He raised his glass in admiration. 'Am I glad that those two young colleagues of yours have disappeared? They were fun for a while but they are not in your league.'

Sylvia nearly choked on her wine when he continued; 'I will tell my pal how good you are. He is planning to come along in a few days time.'

The nest day when she arrived at the salon she was surprised to see Fred standing outside, by the door. He looked extremely agitated. He rattled the handle and kicked hard against the door.

'See what that bastard has been up to. He changed the locks last night, including the one on the back door.' He gave her a weak smile. 'I don't know how long this will take to sort out. I must call my lawyer. Sorry Sylvia, but you had better take the day off. When I have solved the problem I'll give you a call.' In frustration he gave the door another kick. 'Let's go. I will give you a lift to the metro station.'

Sylvia was glad of the chance to take the day off and, although she sympathised with Fred, she felt the need to escape from all the aggravation. She decided to spend the day shopping in the centre of Rotterdam, and was soon absorbed in one of her favourite past times, meandering through the busy shopping precincts full of boutiques, shoe shops, cafes and people.

It was not her intention to buy anything, but of course the inevitable happened. A sexy, red party dress elegantly posed on a dummy in one of the windows caught her eye, and a few minutes later she was standing before a full length mirror admiring her reflection.

'Madam! It fits you perfectly,' exclaimed the sales lady, clapping her hands in enthusiasm. 'I wish I had a figure like yours. You look gorgeous. It was made for you.'

Sylvia was trapped, and for the next couple of hours she had a purpose in her shopping, finding some perfectly matching shoes.

Time for lunch, she thought, as she dropped her colourful plastic bags on to the chair next to her. She had slowly worked her way up to the top floor of the most exclusive department store in Rotterdam, and could not resist taking lunch in their rooftop restaurant. She ordered a salmon salad and coffee and felt happy and contented as she eased back in her chair to admire the panoramic view through the window.

She had just finished her coffee when the waitress appeared and placed glass of white wine in front of her.

'I didn't order that,' she protested.

'It's from your friends over there,' the waitress smiled, pointing to two smartly dressed young men sitting at a nearby table.

They smiled at her and raised their own glasses, but made no attempt to join her.

Ever since her early teens she had been aware of her attraction to men, and was used to their uninvited attentions. She felt flattered that her efforts to look glamorous were appreciated. The two men looked harmless and were obviously escaping for lunch from their boring work in some nearby office. She raised the glass and smiled back.

When she had finished the wine she paid her bill and picked up her bags to leave.

'Thanks for the wine,' she said cheerfully, when she reached their table.

'You brightened up our day,' said one of them, cheekily. 'May we ask your name?'

'It's on here,' she answered, leaning forward provocatively and sliding two of her business cards into the top pocket of his jacket. 'Have a nice afternoon at the office.'

Still feeling in a mood for pampering herself, she made her way to her favourite hairdresser to get her hair washed and styled.

The next morning she was woken out of a deep sleep by the penetrating, repetitive noise of her mobile ring tone.

'It's Fred here. Sorry to disturb you so early, but I have some good news for a change.' He sounded cheerful. 'The salon is open again.'

'How did you manage that?' she asked, trying to focus her mind.

'My lawyer put Hans straight and threatened that he would have to pay damages of 500 euros a day until I got access again. He is obviously not too sure of his position, as he quickly sent a messenger to me with the new keys. He was apparently too embarrassed to come himself.' He sounded relieved. Can I rely on you turning up today?

'Of course Fred. I'll be along as usual.'

She smiled to herself at the thought of the mighty Hans having to back down. But she realised that Fred was still in a weak position being months behind with the rent, and wondered how much longer he could really survive.

When she arrived at the salon Fred and Anita were already there. Fred jumped up to welcome her with outstretched arms. She was one of his few allies left, in his battle against the evil Hans. He quickly poured her and Anita some coffee and himself a glass of beer.

Anita was looking anxious. 'Hans contacted me this morning, she said, in a trembling voice. 'He said that the takeover will take place today.'

'Then what happens?' asked Sylvia.

''We don't know. It's in the hands of our lawyer. He is pretty smart. Let's hope he works something out. All we can do is sit and wait for the outcome.'

Fortunately for Sylvia a pleasant looking man walked in, and for a while she could escape and get some amusement from doing what she had become good at; chatting to, arousing, and relieving some charming but desperate men.

Each time she returned to the bar she could sense the agony that Fred and Anita were going through. She tried to cheer them up with some irrelevant chit chat, but every time the phone rang or the door opened, they nearly had nervous breakdowns.

As the hours passed Fred became more agitated. The empty beer cans and the full ashtray were evidence of his desperation. Eventually he could stand it no longer. He gave a sigh of frustration, went to his office and dialled his lawyer.

'Are you sure?' They heard him stutter. 'Does that mean......?'

It was quiet for a few minutes then they heard the phone being slammed down

'Anita! He shouted,' rushing out of his office and grabbing her in his arms. 'It's over. It's over. She didn't turn up. Hans sat waiting for hours but Nancy didn't turn up. In the end his lawyer called her aunt who told him she had decided, rather suddenly, to take a holiday in Tenerife for a couple of weeks.'

'So she backed out of the deal?' Asked Anita, looking incredibly relieved.

'Well, whether she really inherited any money or not, is not clear. Maybe she was just living out a fantasy. Anyway! Hans got what he deserved, a big shock. He probably won't bother us again for a long time,' said Fred, grabbing a bottle of wine. 'Come on Sylvia. Let's all celebrate.'

183

Over the next few weeks business began to pick up. Fred had recovered his self confidence and had smartened up his appearance. He had paid a visit to the hairdresser's and was wearing a new dark grey suit and black shirt. With some persuasive advertising he finally succeeded in finding several new attractive young ladies.

Anita was also more enthusiastic and turned up regularly. From all the stress she had been through she had lost several pounds and was now her old glamorous slimmed down self, happy to help behind the bar and charm the customers. Sylvia helped her think up some more enticing adverts to attract the customers, using both the local newspapers and the internet. She had also discovered that one of her favourite regulars was a website expert and had persuaded him to improve their website in exchange for a few free sessions with her.

Fred had decided not to repeat the Special Saturday party. It had been a bit too wild. Instead he had found ways to make the salon available for private parties, with or without the services of the girls.

Now that Anita was back in action there was little need for Nanno. Fortunately he was busy with his DJ work and rapidly losing interest, especially as Fred persuaded him to return his keys and charged him the full rate if he wished to make use of any of the girl's services.

Sylvia began to enjoy the livelier atmosphere in the salon and the company of the new girls. She even enjoyed helping out the beginners. She realised that they were not a threat to her and that the more choice available to the clients, the better it was for the business. It improved the salon's reputation. It was almost like old times when they had first opened, except that now she was the one with all the experience, admired by the other girls. She was still the top performer and had enough clients to keep her busy every day.

Sometimes during a quiet moment she would close her eyes and think about her present situation, and fantasise about what the future had in store. She was getting restless and could not envisage doing this work forever. Although she was having fun it was not such a challenge any more, it was becoming routine. Subconsciously she was missing something. Did she need a new escapade, or was it real romance she was yearning for, falling for someone she could admire. Someone she could share her innermost thoughts with and make plans with.

Late one afternoon when she returned to the bar, after an hour's session with one of her regulars, Sylvia was surprised to find Fred filling champagne glasses and Anita handing out cream cakes to everybody.

'What's the special occasion?' she asked.

They were all looking at her with big smiles.

'It's from one of your admirers,' answered Anita. 'He's waiting for you in the office.'

Sylvia's heart missed a beat. *Who could it possibly be? Why is he hiding in the office?* She instinctively straightened her skirt and fluffed up her hair with her hands as she went towards the office. Her heart was pounding. As she pushed open the door she instantly recognised the deep voice that was softly singing; *Sur le pont, d'Avignon -- on y danse -- on y danse------------------*.

She nearly fainted with excitement.

'Erik! It's you! At last!' She cried. 'What are you doing here?'

He jumped up, took her in his arms and squeezed her passionately.

'I've come to get you. I've persuaded Fred to let you off this evening so that I can take you out to dinner.' He paused, dropped his arms and looked into her eyes. 'That is, if you are still interested? I realise that I have a lot of explaining to do.'

'Of course I'm interested,' she answered, trying to hide her emotional confusion. 'Why don't you go and join the others while I change into something more respectful. I won't take long.'

All eyes were watching them closely as they put on their coats and made their way to the door.

'Have a nice evening.' said Fred, feeling obliged to be pleasant. 'But, don't forget Sylvia, I expect to see you back on time tomorrow morning.'

Once they had closed the door behind them, they simultaneously breathed a sigh of relief.

'A born slave driver,' muttered Erik, putting his arm round her shoulder and leading her to his car.

'Where are we going?' she asked, as he started the engine, checked his rear view mirror and moved out into the traffic.

186

'It's a surprise. Just relax and enjoy the ride. I will explain everything when get there.'

He stretched his arm over to the back seat and retrieved a plaid car blanket. 'Put this round your legs until the car warms up. You have a short skirt and it's quite chilly.'

'What a gentleman. Are you always so attentive to the ladies?'

'When I'm in the mood,' he laughed.

'You mean when it helps you to achieve your objective?'

'You shouldn't be so cynical,' he answered, giving her a sideways glance. 'Maybe that is a result of your life in the salon?'

'I suppose you are not too happy with my work?' She frowned. 'But I enjoy it. It has its ups and downs, but it's all the fun I get at the moment.'

"I realise that,' he continued. 'But for a lady like you there are better ways to enjoy life.'

'She realised she was spoiling the atmosphere and decided not to pursue the discussion.

He turned on some romantic music and she leaned back into the soft upholstery. They left the built up area of Rotterdam as he turned on to the motorway towards The Hague. She noticed his well manicured hands, firmly gripping the steering wheel and the confident look on his handsome face as he concentrated on his driving. She felt in safe hands and began to relax. The motorway lights flashing by had a hypnotic effect and she could not resist closing her eyes.

She opened her eyes again as the car slowed down and he left the motorway. They were heading towards the coast, past brightly lit office buildings, through busy shopping streets, then through endless residential areas.

'Almost there,' he said, smiling at her. 'You must close your eyes again for the last few minutes and only open them when I tell you.'

She found it difficult to resist the temptation to sneak a look, as she sensed the car slowing down, making a few turns and eventually stopping.

His door opened first, then hers. 'You can open your eyes now,' he said, extending his hand to help her out.

She recognised it immediately. They were standing before the most imposing and famous hotel on the coast of Scheveningen. He handed his key to a young man in a coloured uniform and took her arm as they climbed the marble steps to the entrance.

'This is certainly a nice surprise,' she gasped, looking rather overwhelmed. 'But I am not dressed for this sort of place.'

'Don't worry,' he said, squeezing her arm. 'Everything has been arranged.'

The foyer exuded luxury, with enormous chandeliers, an ornately decorated ceiling and large windows giving a panoramic view over the terrace and beach. A grand piano was being softly played in the background.

'Why don't you take a seat while I check the arrangements at the reception?' he said, leading her to a chair near the window.

A few minutes later he returned, followed by a pleasant looking woman wearing a hotel uniform.

'This is Bernadette. If you would like to go with her she will show you where you can freshen up and change into something more appropriate.'

'But, you know I don't have any other clothes with me.' She felt embarrassed and a little out of place.

'As I told you, that's not a problem.' He said reassuringly. 'I only hope you find everything to your liking.'

With a mixture of curiosity and excitement she followed Bernadette, first to the lift, then to a room on the first floor.

As she passed the plastic key through the slot on the door and pushed it open Bernadette smiled at Sylvia. 'I have been helping Monsieur Vanderbilt for several days to prepare for this evening,' she said, with a rather mischievous look on her face. 'He must be very fond of you.'

Sylvia smiled at her without answering, realising with a shock that this was the first time she had heard Erik's surname.

Her eyes swept round the room with amazement, the thick cream coloured carpet, the rose tinted walls, the heavy maroon curtains framing the view over the sea, and the large bed covered in red satin with red cushions.

Some toiletries had been neatly arranged on an ornate dressing table with a large mirror, including a hair brush and comb, some make up and a bottle of perfume. Lying over the side of the bed was a dark red evening gown, and next to the gown was a pair of matching high heel shoes and an evening bag.

'Monsieur told me that he has a few business calls to make and that you have plenty of time to bathe and dress. When you have finished you can leave any of your possessions that you don't want to take with you, in this room. Just take this pass key with you when you leave, the door will close

188

automatically.' She laid the plastic card on the bedside table.

When the door closed, Sylvia kicked off her shoes and danced round the room. She picked up the dress, held it in front of her and posed in front of the mirror. *Perfect!* She threw the dress on the bed, grabbed the bottle of perfume and sprayed her hair. *Miss Dior, one of my favourites.*

While the bath was filling she sniffed the selection of coloured aromatic liquids on the wash table and poured some into the water. She threw off her clothes, turned on the radio behind the bed and tuned in to some romantic orchestral music, then slid into the warm sea of bubbles.

She was in another world. She smiled to herself, *if only Fred, Anita, Hans, Nanno and all the other people trying to control her life could see her now!*

After twenty minutes day dreaming, she stepped out of the bath, wrapped herself in a bath towel and brushed her hair while stood under the blow drier. Then she sat at the table, touched up her make up and sprayed her body generously with Miss Dior. She put on the gown and shoes and pranced around in front of the mirror to appreciate the result. The gown fitted her perfectly and the low décolleté accentuated her well formed breasts.

A gentle knock-knock on the door brought her back to earth. It was Bernadette.

'Sorry to disturb you Madam, but Monsieur Vanderbilt asked me to check if you were ready. He is waiting in the dining room.' She couldn't resist staring in admiration. 'If I may say so madam, you look really wonderful and the dress fits you perfectly. If you would like to follow me I will show you the way.'

She noticed that Erik had changed into a dinner jacket as he stood up and helped her take her place at the table. It was in a secluded alcove with a view over the sea. A dull red sun was hovering above the horizon.

His eyes were sparkling as he took his seat opposite her. 'You look gorgeous, just as I imagined. The dress was made for you.'

He hesitated, and she realised he was slightly nervous. He cleared his throat before continuing.

'I hope you don't mind me being so presumptuous in making all these arrangements, I just wanted everything to be perfect. I want us to have a perfect evening, but first I have some explaining to do.'

'Why don't we relax and have a glass of wine.' She suggested, trying to put him at ease. She signalled to the waiter.

'Well,' he said, as they watched the waiter pour out some white wine. 'I know I should have contacted you earlier, but I have had some personal problems to sort out.'

'Marriage problems, I suppose.' Sylvia began to feel uncomfortable. 'Are you married?'

'I was, officially that is, but we had been separated for three years. She had moved in with a previous business partner of mine and had no intention of coming back. Two years ago they moved to the States and I lost contact, until recently. A few months ago she contacted me asking for a divorce. She was expecting, for the first time, and wanted to remarry.'

'So! Are you a free man now?'

'Fortunately! yes.' He gave a sigh of relief. 'Free as a bird.'

'Well then,' said Sylvia, reaching out and touching his hand. 'Everything is perfect. I don't have any commitments either.' She raised her glass. 'Let's enjoy the evening, let's celebrate.'

'That's what we are here for,' he nodded, looking his cheerful self again 'Life is for the present and for the future, not for the past.'

'Now, with all this talking I am neglecting you again.' He said, picking up the menu cards and handing one to her. 'You must be starving. Shall we decide what to eat?'

'Nothing too heavy for me.' said Sylvia scrutinising the menu. 'I'd like to start with the lobster soup, and for the main course I would like the sole meunière.'

'I'll join you with the soup, but then I fancy something more substantial. I'll take the chateaubriand.' He nodded to the waiter.

As they took their time enjoying the dinner, they became more and more relaxed. During the first course they chatted about their past experiences. During the second course they discussed their likes, dislikes and future plans. By the time they reached the coffee they were joking and laughing like old friends.

'Now to be serious again,' he said, leaning closer to her. 'I have been in emotional turmoil since our first meeting. You must have put a spell on me. I think about you non-stop and, to be honest, I want to take you away from that place where you work.' He paused to put his hand in his pocket. 'I have something for you.'

Sylvia's heart missed a beat when he took out of his pocket a little fancy box. *Was this the magical moment every woman dreams about? Was*

190

she going to be faced with the most crucial decision in her life? Her heart was pounding rapidly, she was lost for words, but she did not resist as he opened the box, took out a ring, took her hand and placed it on her finger.

'I know this is rather sudden, but I want you think about a permanent relationship with me? He paused for a few seconds. 'But, I don't want you to answer immediately, I want to give you time, and if you agree I'd like to take you on holiday so that we can get to know each other better.'

Sylvia was surprised, excited and almost overwhelmed. She was relieved that he had not made a formal proposal and forced her into a 'yes or no' decision. He was giving her time to make sure. The expression '*marry in haste and repent at leisure*', flashed through her mind.

'That's beautiful, a diamond ring.' she raised her hand to examine the ring closer, then smiled at him. 'Of course, I'd like nothing better than to go on holiday with you.'

She Picked up her evening bag, took out her plastic door key and waved it under his chin. 'Let's go to my room and discuss your holiday plans in more detail.'

A month later, Fred was sorting his mail when he found the card from Bermuda.

Hello Fred and Anita,
Sorry to have disappeared so suddenly, but I have found the
man of my life. I wish you every success with the business.
Fond affection,
Mrs Sylvia Vanderbilt.

Fred stared at the card for a few minutes, picked up a black felt tip pen and wrote along the bottom, *Is this Sylvia's last escapade???* Then he pinned it on the wall next to the coffee machine.

END

www.ingramcontent.com/pod-product-compliance
Lightning Source LLC
Chambersburg PA
CBHW071208260626
47162CB00004B/1224